ALCHEMY OF COURAGE

ALCHEMY OF COURAGE

2026 FICTION FANTASTIC YOUNG WRITERS WINNERS ANTHOLOGY

Alchemy of Courage
2026 Fiction Fantastic Young Writers Winners Anthology
Copyright © 2026 by Wordcrafters in Eugene

Printed in the United States of America

Wordcrafters in Eugene
434 Charnelton, Ste. 102
Eugene, OR 97401
wordcrafters.org

ISBN: 978-1-964193-04-5

Wordcrafters in Eugene

Our Mission

We believe in the power of story. Stories tell us who we are, and who we can be. Wordcrafters empowers writers and readers by increasing access to community, craft, and inspiration. We provide a home for sharing knowledge and stories with each other and future generations to cultivate a more empathetic, creative, and courageous world.

Our Vision

At Wordcrafters, we believe in the power of storytelling and its ability to create community. Wordcrafters works to expand access to who gets to call themselves a writer, to disrupt the gatekeeping around storytelling, and advocate for and celebrate vibrantly diverse voices, especially those that have been marginalized and excluded. We believe channeling the power of our creative voices creates braver, more empathetic, and more equitable places to live.

(+ all the chocolate your writer-heart needs.)

Wordcrafters in Eugene

Staff

Daryll Lynne Evans, Executive Director

Jeaux Bartlett, Associate Director

Jorah LaFleur, WITS Coordinator & Teaching Artist

Audrey Quinn, Marketing Wordsmith

Board of Directors

Phosphor Emery Alethes, President

Eric Braman, Vice President

Carla Orcutt, Treasurer

Annette Marcus, Secretary

Anthology Staff

Daryll Lynne Evans, Jeaux Bartlett

Individual Donors & Members

Karen Abbey
Amanda Adams
Justin Ahrenholtz
Dennis Albers
Phosphor Emery Alethes
Billie Allen
Regina Allen
Laura Allen
Gerri Almand
Jennifer Anderson
K.G. Anderson
Sarita Angulo
Maxwell Aronsohn
Miranda Atkinson
Papa Awori
Nanci Axelton
Stephanie Axley-Cordial
Alyssa Babin
Mark Barbour
Crissy Bartell
Jeaux Bartlett
Mary Bartlett
Aryn Bartley
Taro Baugnon
Mark Beardsley
Kate Beck
Elizabeth Beechwood
Theresa Bergman
Billie Best
Amanda Bird
Korrin Bishop

Laurie Black
Bas Blankenstijn
Mariah Block
John Blyler
Jeffrey Boerst
Bernadette Bourassa
Mia Bowman
Jayna Braden
Heron Brae
Greg Braman
Eric Braman
Rose Brant
Valerie Brooks
Lola Broomberg
Thomas Bunker
AnJanette Burchett
Joshua Burstein
Karyn Byler
Jessica Cagle Faber
Sara Cakebread
Paul Calandrino
Bill Cameron
Greg Cantwell
Phil Carson
Skyler Charbonneau
JB Christy
Kerin Claeson
Leslie Clark
Trena Cleland
Trina Connolly-Fairchild
Shasti Conrad

Simone Cooper
Liane Cordes
Seraph Cortez
Patricia Crisafulli
Mary Cryns
Paul Dage
Jennifer Daniels
Marty Davis
Anne Dean
Tom DeLigio
Denise-Christine
Carol Dennis
Melissa Denny
Angela DeRoos
Liam Despain
Peter Dudley
Elizabeth Dykstra
Kelly Eastlund
Laura Ege
Amy Elliott
Scott Elliott
Tristan Elliott
Vicki Elmer
Daryll Lynne Evans
Bryan Fagan
Elisabeth Fairbanks
Ivy Fife
Matthew Fioti
Savanah Forster
Chance Fortune
Ellen Furstner
Reed Gabrielsen
Liz Gabrielsen
Denise Gaskin
Gloria Geiser
Miriam Gershow

Amalia Gladhart
Bonnie Glass
Nicolas Gold
Henry Goswick
Mitchell Santine Gould
Nicole Grant
Lynda Green
Kai Haddon
Jackie Hall
Yohann Hall
Marjory Hamann
Austin Hampshire
Marilyn Hanes
Annika Phoenix Hanson
Shannon Hart
Becky Harwood
Kim Hatch
Bryan Haynes
Holli Hebl
Marietta Hedges
Char Heitman
Nika Helmer
Brynna Hendrick
Patricia Henley
Jen Hernandez
DeAnn Herringshaw
Taylor Hertz
Alma Hesus
Kara Hirano
Sara Hoadley
William Holden
Stevenmikel Hoy
Marilyn Hull
Saumya Humpf
Brian Hurt
Jonas Hurt

Laura Illig
Shirley Ingram
Cameron Jackson
Janice Jensen
Isabella Jetten
Sarah Johnnes
Raymond Johnson
Mark Jordan
Kali Kardas
Sondra Kelly-Green
Sunshine M Kesey
Mike Kiley
Linda Klein
Heather Kliever
Paul Klippel
Nicole Kuhl
Rosanna Kyniston
Sarah Lame
Laine Lamping
Alex Langeberg
Cori Larson
Peggy Laurance
Emma Serena Lavin
Christina Lay
Helga Lay
Jade Lazaris
Antoinette LeCouteur
Susie Leo
Ben Lilley
Jane Lincoln
Kristine Lodge
Linda Lovick
Yvonne Lyles
Elizabeth Lyon
Lisa MacGregor
Dana Magliari

RoseMarie Malmrose
Annette Marcus
Heather McBride
Chris McDonald
Jordin McDowell
Andrew Mcivor
Jason Mekeel
Bob and Sara Meltebeke
Juliet Meredith
Joshua Mertz
Phillip Merwin
Kevin Michael
Lori Ella Miller
Adam Miller
Heather Mills
Jamie Moffitt
Cal Montgomery
Alisha Moreno
Sammie Morris
Leah Murray
Rosa Myers
Di Nadeau
David Nash
Aspen Navarro
Santiago Navia
Greg Needham
Melissa Nelson
Celeste Nelson
Tammy Nezol
Liz Nichols
Rosemary Nigro
Nina Nolen
Darcy Nolte
Justine Norton-Kertson
Eileen O'Brien
Eileen O'Malley-Hanna

Chris O'Neill
Carla Orcutt
Julianna Ormsby
Cheryl Owen-Wilson
Sarah Paige
Susan Palmer
Shiela Pardee
Tai Passaretti
Erin Pasternack
Paul Pastrone
Sandi Pattison
Kimberlie Payne
Sarah Peters
Debbie Pfeiffer
Lain Pierce
Sue Pileggi
Laura Poff
Julie Polhemus
Elaine Power
Elayne Puzan
Emily Pyle
Deb Quinn
Erin Radniecki
Laura Ray
Dylan Redd
Emily Reed
Lori Reed
Laurie Reed
Kim Reeder
Grace Richards
Philip Robbins
Victoria Robinson
Ken Robinson
Brandy Rodtsbrooks
Holly Russell
Jane Rygg

Jill Sager
Ellen Saunders
Lexi Scanlon
Melia Scanlon
Cynthius Scanlon
Susan Schneider
Joachim Schulz
Bruce Sedgwick
Jonathan Seidel
Marianne Senhouse
Athena Shah-Scarborough
Gilda Sheppard
Lydia Shipway
Sage Silverstein
Roni Slye
Jean Snider
David Snider
David Solbach
Jeremy Speaks
James Stegall
Jonathan Steinke
Barb Stevens-Newcomb
Autumn Sturtz
Nasim Talebreza-May
Violetta Tarpinian
Carol Taylor
Wendy Thelander
Akiko Thomas
Kathy Thomas
Barbara Tobin
Andy Traisman
William Trevarrow
Gabriel Trout
Annie Tupek
Anne Turner
Rebecca Tursa

Jess Ubel
Rachel Ulrich
Noelle Unterberger
Lois Van Leer
Shannyn Vandevate
Meredith Venneman
Stephen Venneman
Jodi Wainwright
Zachary Wallmark
Aldis Weible

Julia Weldon
Ryan Werthwein
Sue Wielesek
Erin J. Wolff
Rachael Wolfgang
Elli Work
Tommie Yeo
Summer Young-Jelinek
Deha Zehava
Rhonda Zimlich

Sponsors

Euphoria Chocolate Company

James F. and Marion L. Miller Foundation

Luminare Press

Marie Lanfrom Charitable Foundation

MillsDavis Foundation

Oregon Arts Commission

Smith Family Books

CONTENTS

The Courage to Feel

The Courage to Act

The Courage to Be

The Courage to Remember

INTRODUCTION

It takes courage to grow up and become who you really are.

—*e. e. cummings*

The past six years have been…a lot. For all us, yes, but for youth the trials and tribulations of a pandemic, wild fires, political and social upheaval, economic instability, and now war hit particularly hard. Could we blame them if they retreated into fear?

And yet, we believe that in spite of (maybe because of?) all the challenges they face, today's youth do have the courage to, as e.e. cummings says, grow up and become who they really are.

In *Alchemy of Courage*, these fifteen young writers have transmuted their many uncertainties, frustrations, and fears into stories of hope, of exploring identity, of silliness and of seriousness; of friendships, of overcoming challenges great and small, and of making mistakes and having the courage to own and correct them.

We believe these youth will lead the way to a future full of creativity, resilience, and—most importantly—hope.

Fiction Fantastic remains one of the few opportunities in Lane County to showcase student writing or provide creative writing instruction. In our thirteenth year of the contest in 2026, 89 entries poured in from 30 schools (public, private, and home-school) across Lane County, young writers took part in creative writing workshops, and—thanks to Luminare Press—young writers get to see their words in print in the Winners Anthology!

The selection process is highly competitive for Fiction Fantastic. First, stories go through multiple rounds of blind judging, read by a panel of twenty-five volunteer judges made up of writers, educators, and community members. Then the top stories in each grade grouping go to our editors (still without identifying student info), who select the winning stories and placements. Finalists learn their placement at the Fiction Fantastic awards ceremony, where they also get to share a short reading from their work.

We cannot do this work without the tremendous support of our community of writers, educators, volunteers, and parents, not to mention the foundations, local businesses, and donors like you who support our youth programs.

Fiction Fantastic is a part of our programs for young writers. Wordcrafters in Eugene has built a strong foundation to serve youth. Since its launch, Wordcrafters has served over 9,000 students across Lane County, including schools in rural and under-served areas. Young writers programs include a monthly Write Club, creative writing summer camps, school assemblies, and more.

This anthology illustrates the power of imagination and the importance of story, particularly in trying times. Join us as we continue to nurture our young writers and future storytellers so that they, in turn, have the courage to dream up the stories of resilience, hope, and fortitude we need to face the challenges life presents us. Read on!

Sincerely,

Daryll Lynne Evans, Executive Director
Wordcrafters in Eugene

2026 Fiction Fantastic Winners

K-2 Spotlight

"The Flying Cats" by Fiona Stacey, Fairfield Elementary School

Elementary school

1st: "Through My Eyes" by Emma Juul, Gilham Elementary School

2nd: "All Mixed Up" by Emmalee Naylor, Gilham Elementary School

3rd: "The Missing Pipsqueak" by Hazel Rallen and Autumn Mooney, Ridgeline Montessori

Honorable Mention: "The House That Watched" by Julia Thompson-Mueller, Ridgeline Montessori

Middle School

1st: "Red Brick House" by Sala Crabtree, Homeschool/Independent Study

2nd: "Sinking" by Cora Fortenbach, Cal Young Middle School

3rd: "Cœur du Clocher" by David Sammons, Spencer Butte Middle School

Honorable Mention: "Rose and the Fairy" by Edmund Titus, Bridge Charter Academy

Honorable Mention: "A Splash of Shadows in a Field of Light" by Lily Maierhoffer, Thurston Middle School

High School

1st: "In Living Memory" by Keiko Weible, South Eugene
High School
2nd: "Autopilot" by Isaac Chou, South Eugene High School
3rd: "The Girl Who Learned the Names of Light" by Arya
Metz-Hogan, Willamette Leadership Academy
Honorable Mention: "Myself, Truly" by Kendall Moeller,
Elmira High School

Editors' Note

"[I]f you can learn a simple trick, Scout, you'll get along a lot better with all kinds of folks. You never really understand a person until you consider things from his point of view [...] until you climb into his skin and walk around in it."

—Atticus Finch in To Kill a Mockingbird
by Harper Lee

Fair warning, Dear Reader.

The stories you're about to read are those of young writers finding their voice and telling their stories. At Wordcrafters, we are firm believers in giving young writers the space to share their stories and learn their voices matter. While we edit for clarity and style, we do not censor student work. In these stories, the authors poke, prod, and push boundaries; conduct thought experiments and explorations of style and genre; and try on other perspectives and ways of being in the world. There are definitely a few swear words, some challenging themes and material, and occasionally a few stumbles as these authors work out the many nuances of, as Atticus Finch puts it, climbing into another's skin and walking around in it—exactly what we hope for from these curious, inventive writers engaging with their world!

The Courage to Feel

RED BRICK HOUSE

BY SALA CRABTREE

Homeschool/Independent Study

T he house smelled of candied hazelnuts, and Christmas carols played from a gramophone in the living room. Papa was in the kitchen making waffles when Liza and Beth entered.

"Get a good workout?" Papa asked Liza, sliding her a cup of coffee across the table.

"Yes. Thank you for this coffee. It's delicious!"

"You are very welcome," said Papa, ruffling Liza's short hair. "What about you, Beth? Get a good sleep?"

Beth accepted a cup of coffee drowsily.

"In France, Liza has to jog up four flights of stairs to wake me up."

"And I still make it to class on time." Liza grinned.

Drawn by the delicious smell of waffles, the late sleepers arrived. Mama immediately gestured for a cup of coffee, looking as though she had hardly slept. But nine-year-old Oliver looked quite refreshed. He appeared to have brought his entire collection of stuffies downstairs with him.

"Merry Christmas Eve!" he called, just to hear "Merry Christmas Eve!" back. Breakfast was served, and everyone tucked into the waffles and orange juice set out by Papa. And that is how Christmas Eve began in the house of red brick.

* * *

Voices drifted to Fender's ears through the open kitchen door. Fender was of average height for a mouse (which was good, because Fender was a mouse). He had fairly large ears and a long, whipping tail. Fender spent a lot of time around the family, and he liked to perform small jobs for them. At the moment, he was pushing a fallen ornament across the floor with the help of Lavender, his best friend and sister. Lavender was rat-like in appearance, with slick, black fur and gentle, brown eyes.

Having reached the trunk of the Christmas tree, they both paused to rest.

"I wish Liza and Beth weren't leaving day after Christmas," said Lavender. Fender wholeheartedly agreed. Liza and Beth, twins, were home visiting for Christmas before returning to their college in France.

"It's never the same here without them," said Fender forlornly.

"I think that's far enough," said Lavender decisively.

"What?!" Fender was incredulous. "We have to get it back to its branch!"

"It was really high up, though," said Lavender uncertainly.

Fender sighed.

"It will be safer than going back the way we came," he pointed out. "The branches will hide us from view."

Lavender bit her lip, torn between a fear of humans and a fear of heights. At last, fear of humans won. She tied the ornament to the ribbon on Fender's tail. All of Fender's twenty-two siblings wore a ribbon on the ends of their tails so that their mother could tell them apart. Fender's ribbon was gold, and Lavender's, of course, was lavender.

With the ornament secured to his tail, Fender leaped into the tree, with Lavender right behind him. They leapt from branch to branch, and soon the pace became methodical. Lavender's tail began to droop, and her muscles began to ache from weariness. Finally, Fender called a halt. They both collapsed onto a sturdy limb.

Looking around, Lavender observed that the pine needles seemed to make a little cocoon around them. The foliage under their tails was so thick it almost looked like a solid floor. Almost. Still, she felt much safer not being able to see the drop.

* * *

After breakfast, Beth insisted that Liza bring down her things so they could start packing. She spread everything out on the living room table and started checking that they had all the necessary identification to travel internationally. After a while, she headed into the kitchen to get a snack.

Pandemonium greeted her. Flour coated the floor, punctuated by sticky egg-and-honey footprints. The table was covered in baking sheets and bowls of cookie dough. A lake of spilled milk covered the counter, and egg shells dotted every surface. Liza and their mother stopped singing Christmas carols at the top of their lungs and stood sheepishly in the center of all the chaos. Beth sighed in resignation. She ducked back into the living room and put the train tickets she was holding on a high shelf out of danger. And then she got to work.

* * *

Carefully, Fender climbed out onto the skinny branches at the top of the tree and shimmied up the nearly bare trunk. Balancing precariously on the last tiny branch, Fender made a flying leap. He landed on the head of the angel, untied the ornament, and hung it up just below him. Then he looped the ribbon around the neck of the angel and tied a complicated knot before lowering the end of the it. A short while after the end had disappeared into the dense foliage, Fender felt a tug and knew the ribbon had reached Lavender. Fender began to heave on the ribbon, throwing all his weight into the task. After a moment, Lavender came into view, clinging with all four paws and tail, her eyes squeezed shut. After some whimpering from Lavender and some perspiration from Fender, Lavender scrambled onto the angel and hugged its neck with all her might, eyes still shut tight. Fender surveyed the living room spread out below them.

"Lavender!" he cried. "Look, it's amazing!"

Lavender peeked from between her fingers. She moaned and covered her eyes again. Something caught Fender's eye. From his high vantage point, he could see the two tickets resting on the shelf to their right.

"Hey, Lavender, I just had an idea."

"What?" said Lavender, suspiciously. Fender's ideas usually got them into trouble.

"We could take Liza and Beth's train tickets."

"What?! NO! If they don't have the tickets, they can't go back to college! And it would be stealing!"

"It would be borrowing and intentionally not returning, and everyone (including them) is happier when they are at home."

Lavender looked unconvinced.

"Look," said Fender. "You said yourself that you wished they were staying."

"How would we ever get over there?" asked Lavender.

Fender pulled a fishing hook from his bag and tied it onto the end of his ribbon. He swung the line around his head and then let go and watched it soar over the room and catch on the edge of the shelf. He took two paperclips from his bag and threaded them onto the line. Holding onto one with each hand, he instructed Lavender to grasp his tail. This she did, albeit grudgingly. Fender leapt from the head of the angel and flew swiftly through the air, with Lavender holding onto his tail for dear life.

"You could have warned me that we were going to zip line!" Lavender admonished.

"And next time you can try not to squeeze so hard!" Fender retorted. The landing was bumpy, but all in all, the two mice were all right.

"Okay, grab one of the tickets, and I'll grab the other. We've gotta hurry or else Beth will catch us."

"'We'?" asked Lavender skeptically.

"Yes, 'we,'" said Fender with exasperation. "Come on, don't Liza and Beth always talk about how much they miss home? This is for the good of the family. Now are you going to help me or not?"

Reluctantly, Lavender took a train ticket and started to drag it. Together they rappelled down from the shelf and threw the tickets into the crackling fire.

* * *

By the time Beth exited the kitchen, the sink was empty of dirty dishes, the countertop gleamed, and the table was adorned with fresh roses. In the oven, two sheets of cookies were baking, while Liza and her mother mixed frosting. Back in the living room, Beth reached for the tickets to resume packing, but the shelf was empty. She turned slowly and spotted the twin papers curling to ashes in the hearth.

An emergency family meeting was called in the impeccably clean kitchen. Mama had spread out sandwich makings and a full pitcher of lemonade. With laden plates, everyone took their place around the table. Papa looked wearily from face to face.

"Not fifteen minutes ago, someone at this table threw both Liza's and Beth's train tickets into the fire. Not only that, but they also slashed a hole in Liza's only travel bag." There was silence. "If anyone has anything they would like to say, then please come forward."

"Hear! Hear!" said Liza, glaring at Oliver. "There is a traitor in our midst!"

"That's a bit melodramatic, Liza," said Papa. "I don't want to point fingers, but I suggest that whoever the culprit is, they should seriously consider their actions." He paused. "Anything else we should discuss?"

"We need new hinges for the pantry door; it won't close all the way," said Mother.

"And I can't find my phone," said Beth.

"And—"

"All right, meeting adjourned!"

* * *

Crouched in the shadows of the kitchen, the two young mice exchanged glances. Lavender moaned and covered her face with her paws.

"We are in soooo much TROUBLE!" she moaned. Fender wasn't listening.

"But we didn't do anything to her bag," he mused.

"Which means…" Lavender caught on.

"Someone else is trying to stop Liza and Beth from leaving, too."

The mice bounded back through the mouse hole without a backward glance and wound their way through the labyrinthine passageways that honeycombed the area beneath the house. The tunnels, lined with brick and intersected by pipes, gradually transitioned into earthen passageways that twisted, wriggled, and doubled back. Fender navigated with ease. He was at home here among the sandy halls and roots and skittering black beetles.

The rest of Fender's family lived in these tunnels, too. But despite living just beneath their floorboards, they showed little interest in their human hosts. The adult mice often voiced that Fender was crazy to hang around humans so often. Secretly they admired his courage, though they would have no part in it. They only ventured out to scavenge for food. The youngsters, however, always thronged around Fender, asking to hear of his latest exploits and adventures. Throughout the mouse tunnels it was agreed that Fender was uncommonly bold. Lavender, though timid and frightened of humans, also loved each of the upstairs occupants like members of her own family.

When he approached the main living area, with Lavender at his heels, Fender turned off on a little side path that led to a special little hollow he called his "workshop."

"Come on, Lavender! In here!" called Fender.

Lavender fidgeted uncomfortably. "Fender—" she started.

But Fender kept speaking. "I was thinking we could write a note and then put it somewhere for the other guy to find."

"Fender!" said Lavender a little louder.

But Fender just steamrollered on. "It'll be difficult to write, though," Fender mused.

"FENDER!!!!" Lavender shouted.

Fender stared. Never in his whole life had Lavender ever spoken above a timid whisper.

"I don't want to be a part of this anymore," she said firmly.

Fender scoffed. "Lavender, we've been through this. This is for the good of the family."

"You're planning something else, aren't you?" said Lavender, narrowing her eyes.

"It's for the good of the family," Fender repeated.

"No," said Lavender.

"Sorry?" said Fender, not quite believing his abnormally large ears.

"I said no," Lavender snapped. "This is going too far! You do what you want, but I'm out." And with that she turned and skittered back through the tunnels. Fender felt a prick of uncertainty as Lavender's voice echoed in his mind, but he pushed it away—there was work to be done.

He rummaged through his workshop and found an old gum wrapper. He set to work writing a note. When he had finished, it read:

Tonite. 3 a.m. The kitchn
—yore felow saboteer.

Then he scuttled back upstairs to lay the bait.

At three a.m., Fender lay in wait among the shadows of the pantry. He had decided that if one were a saboteur, this would be a very good hiding place. Sure enough, a pocket knife and both Liza's and Beth's phones were shoved between the door and the pantry shelves. No wonder the pantry door wouldn't close.

    Winners Anthology

A message had popped up on the phones' glowing screens:

I am pleased to inform you that you won the art
competition that we held just before Christmas break.
As you are aware, the winners receive free art classes
beginning with the new term. If you are interested,
please give me a call tomorrow, December 24, at the
latest. We look forward to seeing you, Professor Tarter.

Fender felt a sharp pang of guilt. He knew Liza and Beth
would be overjoyed to receive that message. Now it was too
late. The darkness was awful. Simply awful. It was making
Fender think about all the things he had done wrong.

Then he heard the shuffle of slippers, and a flashlight
beam swept the darkness. Oliver appeared, clutching his
stuffed elephant, King Charles III. Fender was not surprised
to see him. The pocket knife he had found had Oliver's scent
all over it.

Fender crept out from the shadows and slid a second
note across the kitchen tiles. It said, "I am Fender." An adult
might have been surprised to find a mouse communicating
with them, but for Oliver, the discovery that animals com-
municate was simply confirmation of something he had
always known.

"Did you see the message?" Oliver asked.

Fender nodded.

Oliver started to cry. "I stole their phones the day before
Christmas Eve. I feel terrible about it. I know they wanted
to win that competition so much. They worked so hard on
their artwork. I'm going to get in so much trouble, and I'm
scared that Liza and Beth will be really angry at me. They're

always leaving me here by myself. Mom works so hard that she doesn't have time to look out for me, and Papa, too. I kept telling myself that I wanted to prove I could be just as brave, but really, I was afraid of them leaving. And now I've messed everything up."

It seemed to Fender that Oliver couldn't stop talking—now that he had started, it was all spilling out. Fender didn't know what to say. He wanted to comfort Oliver, but he felt like crying himself.

Suddenly, a movement in the shadows made Fender turn around. Lavender was creeping across the floor. Fender waited for her to bolt into the safety of the shadows, but she walked right up to Oliver. Oliver bent down his head, and Lavender gave his nose a little pat. It was clearly taking all of her self-control not to bolt. She nudged Oliver a little with her nose, as if to say, "I understand."

There comes a time in the life of any child, human or otherwise, when they realize they are not the only people that matter. And then, they begin to see things from stepping in another's shoes, so to speak. Sometimes this change is very gradual, but it can also be shockingly abrupt. So it was for Fender. Lavender was always scared to do the things that Fender had made her do, but she always did them anyway. Fender was always pushing her to do things out of her comfort zone and then making her feel cowardly for not wanting to do them in the first place. Fender suddenly realized how hard that must have been for Lavender. He smiled at her to show he wasn't angry, and Lavender smiled back. *She's the bravest mouse in the mouse tunnels*, he thought.

And then, quite suddenly, all three realized what they had to do. Fender swallowed. This was going to take a lot of courage.

In the end, they had to break the text back to Professor Tarter into several speech bubbles—it was simply too hard to explain everything in so short a paragraph. In short, they told the Professor everything that had happened over Christmas break and asked if he could please give Liza and Beth the classes anyway, because they knew that Liza and Beth would like them so much. It was 4 o'clock in the morning before they sent it.

With half the battle over, they set their minds to returning Liza and Beth's phones. Kneeling down, Oliver held out his hand so that Fender could scamper up on his shoulder. Lavender timidly stepped out from the shadows too, and Oliver scooped her up and pocketed her before she had a chance to protest. Oliver tiptoed up the stairs; his knowledge of which steps creaked and which didn't was very useful now.

The door to the twins' bedroom swung open noiselessly on its hinges. Oliver crept in, hoping against hope that the twins were asleep. The room was completely dark and silent. He breathed a sigh of relief.

"They're asleep," he whispered. Silently, he headed for the nightstand beside Liza's bed.

Suddenly, the room was bathed in light. Liza was sitting on the lower bunk of the twins' childhood bed. Oliver and the two mice froze. Liza smiled with satisfaction. "Caught red-handed," she said, taking a swig from her half-empty mug.

Oliver took a deep breath. Lavender gave him an encouraging nuzzle from inside his pocket. Starting from the beginning, Oliver told them everything.

* * *

OLIVER RAN DOWNSTAIRS TO OPEN PRESENTS THE MINUTE he woke up. Fender had made his two paper clips into ice skates for Lavender. Lavender gave Fender a new bag with separate compartments for all his things. Oliver got a ticket so the whole family could visit France later that summer. Father got a gramophone to replace the old one. Mother got a laptop so she could work at home from now on.

Liza and Beth both found mysterious gifts in their stockings. Liza found a gold ribbon, and Beth found a lavender one. They also got an email from their college informing them that the classes were still available if they called today. And that is how Christmas started in the house of red brick.

ALL MIXED UP

BY EMMALEE NAYLOR

Gilham Elementary School

Chapter 1: Autumn Andes

Have you ever heard the term "sleep like a baby," but babies don't sleep through the night at all? Or wondered why cookies are *baked* and bacon is *cooked*? Should it be the opposite? Just some thoughts of mine. Well, my baby sister Clarabella cries her face off. I laugh at the thought of the ridiculous image that prints on my mind.

I sit up in my bed to check the time. It reads 11:32. Looks like I won't be getting much sleep. First day of middle school with what looks like a case of pink eye. Darnit.

Click!

"Autumn, time for school!" booms Mom as she switches on the lights.

I shove my face into my pillow. "Ten more minutes, Mom!" My pet dog Floofy licks my face, which makes me open my eyes.

"No honey, now's the time!"

"Fine." I groan. I shoot out of bed once I hear my four-year-old brother Archie playing with my cookbooks. I quickly pull him away from my desk.

"Sissy, no!" he yelps.

I go to the bathroom mirror to check on my disgusting fat pimples. They look like giant mountains, or at least, ugly, fat, bumpy ones.

Archie waddles carrying poor Floofy the wrong way.

"Buddy, don't hold him like that!" I say in an annoyed tone. I've always been embarrassed by Floofy's name because Archie named him the second he could talk.

I comb my hair while humming songs from my mom's Christmas playlist, even though it's still September.

"Autumn! What hairstyle do you want today?" asks Mom.

"How about two braids?"

"Got it," says Mom.

After she's done with my hair, I go choose what to wear. I end up with white sweatpants and Nikes (my new pink and white ones), a cool striped yellow and white sweater, and two bracelets on my wrist.

I devour a toaster waffle, some strawberries, and take a to-go cheese stick. Pack my backpack and hurry off with my mom.

On the drive there, I get just a little nervous. Probably first day of middle school jitters.

Chapter 2: Amber Williams

We're parked in the school parking lot, and I'm looking for Autumn. I really hope I see her.

"Momma, do you see Autumn?"

"No, honey," Momma says. "Have a great day, honey."

"Thanks, Mom! Bye!" I say as I climb out of the car.

I walk through the crowd of people. I call Autumn to see if she is here.

"Hello," says Autumn.

"Are you here yet?" I say into my phone.

"I'm near the sign near the school, you know, like the O'Hena Middle sign!"

"Okay!" I say. "Bye!" I walk to the sign. There she is.

"Hi!" I say.

"Hey," she says back.

"Hey! Pimple girl!" says a familiar voice. Travis Tate! I knew it!

"Shut up!" I say defending Autumn. Oh, how much I hate that guy's straggly hair and burning brown eyes, his sweaty red palms and cheeks. Finally he leaves.

"You know he just wants to pick on you to feel better," I say to Autumn.

"Yeah," she says.

I just don't get why he picks on her. When I look at her, I see silky hair the color of peanut butter, gleaming eyes, one brown and one green, and he just sees the pimples.

Also, she loves cooking and baking. She has literally won the kid's baking championship. I mean the only thing I can cook is eggs and my long braids get all over the food!

"I wonder where Esme is." I say.

Chapter 3: Esme Barnard

I rush through the halls. "Finally, I found you guys!"

"Where were you, Esme?" says Drew.

"I don't really know. My dad took some wrong turn or something!" I say.

"Attention students. School starts in five minutes. Attend your classrooms!" booms Principal Hawkins on the intercom.

"Well, bye guys!" I say.

We all have different homerooms. Amber is the luckiest though. Amber is so outgoing and doesn't care what people think of her. She's so cool with her little braids. Sometimes pink, or blue or brown, or all black and blonde. Her braids are black and then fade into a different color. She says it takes seven hours to do her hair. Sometimes her mom lets her wear centimeter crop tops and put on makeup. She's so cool. And…

"Esme? Esme?"

I look around startled.

"Stop spacing out!"

Oh, it's my teacher Ms. Belhops.

"What is your favorite school subject!?" she booms.

"Well, ummm, I like, ummm, free time?" I say.

"Well, if you want any, stay focused!" she says, embarrassing me.

I go red-cheeked while I watch kids staring, smirking, and slightly laughing about me. Even Travis is eyeing me down. I hate Ms. Belhops with her thick glasses and pursed red lips, her wrinkles head to toe make me want to gag.

I check the time on the clock. 10:13. Lunch is at 12:25. Oh gosh, this is going to be a long day today.

Chapter 4: Autumn Andes

Finally, lunch! I rush down the halls. After lunch means Cooking 101. I love cooking; it is the best! One time I got to go on a show. It was awesome! I got third!

Once I get to the area to order I realize lunch is fish sticks. Eww! I really love fish. I swear they are amazing but just not here. They are slimy and icky, soggy, and I bet microwaved. I can make fish n' chips better than they can I think. I know this amazing tartar sauce recipe.

Or maybe Alaskan cod with garlic lemon butter. That would hit the spot. But this smells like sandy seaweed puked out by a dead fish.

I look for open tables. There! That table has Amber, Esme, and Coby. Coby was in my fifth-grade class. He is nice and he has fluffy hair the color of leather and sand, also light blue eyes.

I sit down. They all stare at me like I'm crazy.

"Hey," I say.

"Oh, yeah, hi," says Coby.

We talk about random stuff. Esme has such a great lunch. Well, a pretty good lunch, better than mine. Obviously, it's some sour cream and onion Lays, McDonalds fries, burger, and chicken nuggets, plus a twinkie. Even though that stuff is good, I'll just eat when I get home.

Esme has very short hair as straight as a line. Nervous yet positive personality, big dimples, and emerald green eyes, tons of freckles, and always wears her hair in pigtails.

After lunch I rush to Cooking 101. I'm so excited. I don't even stop by my locker.

Once I get there I notice a new girl I didn't know at my elementary school.

"Class, meet Faye," says my Cooking 101 teacher, Ms. Lindsay.

"Um, hi" Faye says.

"Tell us something about yourself," says Ms. Lindsay.

"I'm eleven years old. I moved from a small town in Nevada because my dad got a job here in San Diego. Also I love cooking, baking, and reading, also collecting water bottle stickers, and I love my cat Snickerdoodle," she says.

Faye is short and has wavyish blonde hair, thick glasses, braces, and pearl earrings, and tons of backpack keychains. She sits down after she's done talking.

"The top two of you in this class will be able to get into a cooking contest with a prize of two thousand dollars," says Ms. Lindsay.

That's gonna be easy to get in the top two. Bet I'll be winning the contest. I could buy a Nintendo. That would be awesome. I daydream. Bring it on!

"In a week, I will give you a quiz," says Ms. Lindsay.

Chapter 5: Faye Woods

It's been a week. I'm so excited! *I hope I get into the top two*, I think as I walk to Cooking 101.

"OK, class, I'm going to give you all a really hard quiz that some of you might have never heard of."

She gives me the test. I write my name and get started.

Some of the questions are about stuff like butter basting and deep frying. To write step-by-step instructions to make different foods with different things. Like the easiest question is how to make croissants but to me all of the questions are easy. I'm the second person to finish. The first person is this girl named Autumn. She looks pretty nice.

Once everybody's done, Ms. Lindsay looks at her sheet that has all the right answers.

"What a surprise, we have two people who got them all right. Autumn Andes and Faye Woods! Congratulations!"

I'm so happy! Autumn comes over and high-fives me.

"Great job!" she says.

"You, too!" I say back.

After school my dad takes me to my favorite ice cream place. He orders pumpkin pie flavor for a fall twist, and I order pistachio and chocolate.

"Yum!" I say once I take my first lick.

"Your cooking contest is on Sunday, or at least round one," says Dad.

"It's Friday, so not too long" I say.

I get home and read and pet Snickerdoodle until dinner,

then eat some tacos, take a shower, and watch Food Network until bedtime.

I open my eyes while yawning. Morning already? I throw some clothes on, and eat some breakfast and then watch more Food Network with Mom, Dad, and my younger sister Chloe.

I can't wait until tomorrow, so wish me luck! I write in my diary.

Chapter 6: Autumn Andes

It's Sunday! I jump out of bed and go to the mirrors. "Another day, another slay!" I say to my reflection.

My family heads off to the cooking place. All of the people are there already so I must be a little late. I see Faye and about twenty different kids from different schools.

"Hello, everyone!" says a booming voice. "I'm Mr. Joe, one of three judges."

"I'm Ms. Marletts," says a thin woman with pricey designer clothes, the kind of person who would spit out good food.

"Hey, I'm Chef Michael," says, well, Chef Michael. "You are all here for your skill and talent. A winner will win. Others… well, better luck next time. You will have an ingredient you will have to use every time today. That key ingredient is broccoli! You will have one hour to finish. There are stations with names."

"Ready, set, go!" said Mr. Joe.

I rush to my table. I know what I'm making, broccoli cheddar soup in a bread bowl.

"Faye, what are you making?"

"My great grandma's beef and broccoli with rice."

"Yum!" I say.

I gather all of my ingredients for my soup, make some bread, cut a hole in it. Make my soup, pour it in, make it fancy and…

"Time is up!" says Mr. Joe. The judges get their first meal. A rice noodle Thai curry. It's a broccoli curry. They seem to enjoy it but I can't tell that much. The next dish is some air-fried garlic broccoli. Third is just normal broccoli, fourth is Faye's beef and broccoli. Fifth is alfredo with broccoli, and last is mine.

"Yum, very good," they say. And so on with other dishes.

"Today, we will be sending three of you home. After that, there will be seventeen contestants remaining. Okay, Sam, your plain broccoli was not the best. You will be my pick to go," says Ms. Marletts.

"Sorry, Jessi, your garlic broccoli was too crispy and burned," Chef Michael says. "And last, sorry Gabbie, you are a talented cook, but the alfredo was the main dish. The broccoli did not shine," says Mr. Joe. "See you all tomorrow. The next twist is pizza. Cool, fun, get creative!"

Chapter 7: Faye Woods

I wake up bright and early. I know exactly what I'm going to make. I can't go to school. I'm going to skip today so I can cook. I'm going to make deep-fried pizza onion rings! Trust me, they will be delicious!

Once I finish breakfast, I hurry off with my family. I see Autumn when we get there. That's good! I'm so excited because we are kind of friends. Now that's awesome.

Then the judges remind us about the challenge and blah, blah, blah, until they say that we're working in pairs! I rush over to Autumn.

"We're a group!" she says, clarifying.

"Ready, set, NO! Just kidding, GO!" Mr. Joe says. We rush over to our station.

"I know what we can make," says Autumn.

"What?" I say.

"Mini deep-fried calzones."

"Okay," I say. I don't mind. I will just make onion rings another time.

Sometimes I think Autumn can be a little bossy. She wants a Nintendo. I want cooking supplies, but she's just trying to win.

She gathers all of the ingredients and we start. She gets some dough. We make sauce with chopped basil, shredded cheese, and sausages and olives in it. I wrap them up and she deep-fries them.

"That's time!" said Mr. Joe. People bring in their dishes.

"First up, Daniel and Abby," the judges say. They have pizza roll up dippers with ranch. Number two is Cam and Alisha. They have pizza French fries. Next is mini pineapple pizzas, also some Thai curry pizza and dip. Next is ours. They seem to kind of like it.

"We have decided four groups will be eliminated this round. Then there will be nine people left," says Mr. Joe.

"My elimination will be Daniel and Abby. Your dippers were oily," says Ms. Marletts.

"Mine will be Julie and Morgan. The pineapple made it soggy," Mr. Joe says.

"Cam and Alisha, I'm sorry—your sauce was not the best," says Chef Michael.

"And now, we all agree on Charlie and Natasha. Your pizza was good but not prize-worthy," says Mr. Joe.

I'm so happy I hug Autumn. "Want to have a sleepover for tomorrow's competition?" I ask.

"Ah, sure, I think. I've never had one. Let me ask my mom." She calls her mom.

"It's a yes!" she says. We drive back to my home. On the way we stop at Olive Garden for dinner.

Back at my house, we play games, eat kettle corn, peanut butter cups, gummy bears, and sip hot cocoa. Watch Disney movies until we're tired. Right as we start putting pjs on and brushing our teeth my dad comes up.

"Autumn, change of plans. Your mom is picking you up. Now."

Chapter 8: Autumn Andes

Next thing I know I'm in the car. My mom is driving straight-faced.

"What's wrong?" I ask. "Why did you pick me up?"

"Floofy got hit by a car!" she says, tearing up. "I don't have enough money to pay for vet bills. I need money to pay for our food and running water and our car and everything."

I'm shocked. I cry. I'm frozen and heartbroken.

When we get home, I check on Floofy. He's still alive, luckily he only broke his leg. Maybe I can win money to help him. Floofy looks at me with his dachshund eyes filled with sadness. I cry myself to sleep that night, hoping things won't get worse.

Chapter 9: Faye Woods

My dad tells me what happened on the way to the competition. I feel bad and sad for her.

"Hello, children. Today is dessert day. Make desserts," says Mr. Joe. "We will eliminate seven of you. One, two, three, go!"

I'm going to make peanut butter pie. It is such a good recipe plus my favorite food. I make the pie crust, make the filling and…time's up!

First up is brown sugar pecan cookies, two is cookies and cream fudge, three is coconut macaroons, four is lemon poppy seed cake, five is my peanut butter pie, and six is Autumn's dessert. She's made chocolate hazelnut brownie bites with ice cream dip. Seven is red velvet cupcakes, eight is cookie ice cream sandwiches, and nine is candied flower petals.

"The two chefs who will be in the championship round are Autumn Andes and Faye Woods! The Championship is Friday. Good luck!"

Chapter 10: Autumn Andes

Click.

"It's morning," Mom says. "You have school today."

I wake up. No Floofy licking my face. Just the light feeling of nothingness surrounding me. Floofy is snoring in the kitchen.

I get to school. Esme and Amber look different. Esme got contacts! Her hair is in a high pony. They're talking to a group of girls and laughing like best friends.

"Hey, Esme and Amber!" I say going up to them. They walk away going off with Brittany and Charlotte, AKA the mean girls, taking selfies and laughing.

Then I realize my best friend have dumped me.

I'm mostly with Faye that day. Who knew so much could happen in four days?

Chapter 11: Faye Woods

It's the big day of the final competition. I'm excited-ish and nervous-ish.

"Welcome, girls. Cook or bake something special to you. Three, two, one, go!" says Chef Michael.

I'm cooking pizza onion rings, like I said I would.

I gather my ingredients and get started.

Chapter 12: Autumn Andes

I'm cooking Alaskan cod with garlic herb butter. Hope it's the winning bite because I better win for Floofy. I'm his only hope. We finish cooking. Time goes by fast.

"Three, two, one. That's time!" says Ms. Marletts. They try our dishes. "And the winner is…Faye Woods!"

My heart skips a beat. She won and I didn't!

She looks so happy.

"Hey, Autumn" says Faye. "This belongs to you." She hands me the money for Floofy.

Now it is October. Me and Faye trick-or-treat together. We love going to each other's houses, and Floofy is healed. Our favorite thing to do is play our favorite games on my new gift, a Nintendo.

Sinking

by Cora Fortenbach

Cal Young Middle School

"I know lockers shouldn't be this important, but somehow to me it is. It holds my things without yelling or calling me dramatic. It's something small but something I can still rely on. It's the only thing that stays where I left it, opens when I ask it to. Even though the inside smells like gym socks and old papers," was the last thing I wrote when my father ripped the book out of my hands.

"What is this?!" he snapped. I could just smell the aroma of alcohol pierce my nose, like breathing in cold air too fast but with a pungent scent. "Dramatic?! Well maybe if you stop writing stupid poems."

"Dad!" All I can recall after that was the feeling of tears running down my face, warm against the bruises.

I don't remember when I stopped believing that houses could be warm. Maybe it was when I was eight, standing outside, waiting at the door with my ear pressed up against the rough wood with peeling paint, listening.

"I never wanted him in the first place!"

My mom's voice broke midway through. My heart dropped. Little did I know it would never stop dropping, it would just keep on falling. Then came the sound of breaking plates—nothing new.

Since then I have realized my place in this world. I move

like I'm apologizing to the air just for existing, like a mouse waiting for the cat to inevitably wake up. I know things that most kids will never understand—how skin goes silent right before it bruises, or how rage sounds though drywall. Adults like to say kids are resilient when they don't want to face the truth. They say kids bounce back, but they never say how many pieces you bounce back in. Resilient isn't the same as unbroken.

I'm only twelve, but my bones feel older. My heart feels cold. I realized just how cold the day I sat at lunch eating another soggy sandwich, without a thought in my head. Then I saw a tray crash nearby, sending milk splashing across the table. As I turned to see what caused this I saw her—Mia. The only reason I knew her was because we sat in the same math class. I always thought she was another snaky girl who never repeated an outfit while I wore the same gray hoodie with an old pizza stain on it. Now she was on the ground with milk all over herself, tears reddening her face. I felt nothing, jaw steady, still chewing, my eyes locked on my shoes. One thing I've learned is that emotions get you hurt, and emotions other than anger get you hurt worse. Sometimes I wish I could just turn on a switch in my head to be normal, to understand how to feel. I think about how her face looked and how I sat hunched over, eating a sandwich I didn't even like.

It was seventh period. I was sitting at my desk, staring at the clock, my leg bouncing more than usual, counting down the seconds till I had to go home. It was science, which just dragged on about ecosystems. Pretty boring if you ask me. I flinched as the bell blared, which I always do. Loud noises always make me flinch. That was the main reason I got hit.

"Eli, I need to talk to you," Ms. Aaron said quietly. My heart deepened even more. There's a reason I didn't say my name at the start of this story. I hate my name. All I know about it is that it's the worst thing that happened. It reminds me of everything that makes me want to hide in a corner; a reminder that I'm still here, still alive.

"Is everything okay at home?" A simple question that somehow always sounded fake, but this time it felt real instead of like someone reading off a script.

"Um, I, I…I don—" My legs moved faster than my brain. I ran. Was it the opposite direction from my locker? Yes, yes it was. But at that moment I didn't care. All that mattered was getting out of the classroom, out of that school.

That night I was sitting in the shower, thinking about what Ms. Aaron said. "Is everything okay at home?" The words circled around my head, kinda like the water and how it circled the drain.

Instead of saying yes, like a normal person, I ran. I just wanted to yell at the top of my lungs to Ms. Aaron in that stupid classroom. "No! Nothing is ok! I just want to be done!"

That word, done. What did it mean? Done with life? I'm twelve. What did that mean for a twelve-year-old? I felt a tear run down my face. Shame burned behind my eyes—shame for crying, shame for feeling anything at all.

"Get out! You're wasting water!" my dad yelled, with a gurgle in his throat. I stepped out of the shower, drops of water running down my legs. At this point I was sobbing, the type that you can feel deep in your chest, painful almost, but silent. My face was puffy and red.

As I lay in bed, slowly closing my eyes, a soft tear left my face. But I couldn't sleep, so I started to write. "I cried, hard, different. I felt weak, but it was hope. I felt. Instead of doing nothing, instead of looking away with no feeling in my eyes, I cried." I ripped the page out of my journal, if anything it was stupid.

The next morning during third period, Mr. K told us to write a short paragraph about a thought we had never told anyone. Mr. K was odd. No one really liked him. I didn't either. But writing is a way to live a life never thought before. The words started flowing before Mr. K was done talking. As soon as my pencil touched paper, I was flying.

Sometimes all I want to do is sink. Not into my bed, but just sink. It's not being done, but being free from wanting to be done. When you sink, you sink into a place of peace. I don't get to sink to that place. Not until I can find out who I am. Not until I'm allowed to feel. To cry, to smile. To live a life. Until I can be me, I cannot sink.

"Time to turn it in, bell's in two minutes," Mr. K said in his normal "robotic" voice. I stared at my paper. I hadn't thought about what I was writing. I had just let the words flow. I started to breathe heavily. Just like with Ms. Aaron. But I had to turn it in. My face was hot when I was turning it in. I tried to smile, but my face wouldn't cooperate.

In seventh period Ms. Aaron luckily didn't say anything about yesterday.

The next day Mr. K gave back the papers. I got an A- on mine. I never understood why there were minuses along with pluses. It never looked right to me, don't know why. He didn't even look at me when he gave me the paper, which in some ways I was glad about but in others a little mad. I didn't even get a "Good job, Eli."

Fourth period brought new seats. All I thought was, *great. Now I have to hear another disappointed groan from the person who's going to sit next to me.*

Ms. Taylor started again, interrupting me mid-thought. "Starting with the front row, Eli, and right next to him will be Mia."

Mia didn't groan or even acted annoyed. Sometimes when I'm sitting in the courtyard she will sit right across from me and try to peek at what I'm writing. I just hope she doesn't remember that lunch and how I ignored her when she cried, not even acknowledging what was happening. She didn't get mad. But she never seems like she gets mad. All she seems to do is click her pen a lot. It should be more annoying, but somehow it's not.

It was now Thursday, and I almost broke in front of Mia. She slowly slid into her seat.

"You okay?" She said it in the tone that makes your stomach twist because you don't know what to do with it.

I shrugged. "Yeah, fine." My voice cracked at the end.

She watched me for a second, like she could see me quietly breaking inside, even though I was trying to cover it.

"You don't have to pretend all the time, you know."

I felt something tighten in my throat. I didn't want her to talk to me like that. Not with softness. Soft things just break easier.

"I'm not pretending," I snapped through my clenched teeth. "Can you just…not?"

Her smile faded, but she didn't leave. "I'm just saying I get it. My house is loud, too."

This time I looked at her, really looked at her. I looked at her eyes, tired like she went through things most adults would never get. It scared me. Not because she was lying, but because she wasn't. I grabbed my notebook and stuffed it into my binder.

"You don't know, just don't talk to me," I muttered, trying to not let her see the tears forming in my eyes.

Mia put her hands in her pockets. For a second she looked hurt. Then she nodded. "Okay. Sorry."

I tried to tell myself that things were better off this way. Friends just make you open up to take it away from you. But something about her about her—her eyes—told me everything.

I wrote again that night. "Eyes say more than any voice ever could. How they redden at the sight of something sad. Or how they look when they are hiding a secret." I ripped the page out again, but this time I didn't throw it away. I slid it in my pillowcase and went to sleep. That night I didn't let it leave my side. Something about it gave me comfort, I don't know what. But it just did.

I was replaying a moment in my head on my walk to school. The moment had to have been a month or so before I ever talked to Mia. She laughed at something someone said. But it didn't fully reach her eyes. I wonder how had I never noticed that about her. This time my chest hurt in a way that didn't feel like anger.

The day after I had snapped at Mia, school felt louder. Not literally, just—louder in my head. Every voice sounded sharper, every hallway brighter than the previous. Mia didn't talk to me in math, she didn't even look at me. I pretended not to notice or care. She stopped clicking her pen like morse code. Just quiet. Now the silence felt heavier than any noise.

At lunch I walked toward my table, saw the soggy sandwich waiting for me, and something inside me said no. I couldn't go there again, pretending I was made of stone. I didn't want to walk past Mia either. So I turned around before anyone could notice I was even there and headed down the hall. That's how I ended up at the library doors. The library felt like the only place in school that didn't want something from me. No yelling, no bells blaring, no teacher staring too long. Just the soft hum from the librarian while she organized the shelves.

I picked up a random book, I didn't even look at the title, just started reading. But before I could even start I heard the clicking of a pen. I was about to turn around and tell the person to please stop when someone sat next to me. I didn't want to fully look, but before I could even think, I felt a hand on my shoulder. "Eli, I know you don't want to talk, but—"

I cut her off before she could finish. "Mia, you need to know when to stop. You need to know when it's time to quit and let someone just exist without your help." The words were messy, and so were my feelings. I put my stuff away and tried to leave before she could say anything.

"I want to know how to quit!"

My head moved in confusion. "What?"

"The main reason I got in trouble was because I didn't know when to stop."

I sat back down, trying to understand the words I had just heard.

"I know I'm pushy. But you seem like you know. You know what it's like to hate your own name. You know what it's like to want to sink," she said sorely.

"How do you know that?" My tone was shaky.

"Remember when I fell next to you and you did nothing?" she said, not mad, but curious.

"Yes, and I'm sorry. I didn't, well, I don't know, but I can say that I'm sorry." I couldn't quite articulate the right words.

"I saw your eyes, and it reminded me of myself. How I was and still am scared to show my feelings out loud."

I might not remember what I said next. But I do remember the happy tears falling down my face this time. I still feel shame when I cry, but less than before.

Mia and I are friends now. We talk about deep things. The type of things that make your chest sting. But when I'm talking to her, I feel safe, like I matter.

At the end of the year, Mr. K told us to write about our thoughts and if they had changed at all. I wrote softly this time, making sure every word, every letter, was taken care of.

I am now sinking. I have not made it to peace just yet. But I'm done wanting to be done. I have found myself. And all I needed was someone to see who I can be. I might not fully be free, but I am me.

I got an A+.

Cœur du Clocher

by David Sammons

Spencer Butte Middle School

Elénore arrived in Ville Du Clocher in the late afternoon, when the light turned dull, as though the sky itself had been brushed thin. The town slowly revealed itself as the train descended the hill, stone buildings rising in small clusters around thin streets. At first glance, it looked like any other European town, quiet and orderly, aging and worn out. Only when the road curved inward did she see the clock tower.

The clock tower stood in the town's center, much taller than any of the surrounding roofs, its stone darkened with centuries of rain and smoke. The clock face caught the light in a way that almost felt unnatural, not reflective but luminous, as if the glass held something lit from behind. She studied it longer than she meant to, unsettled not by its appearance but by how easily the town seemed to organize itself around it.

The bells rang as the train pulled to a stop.

The sound was deep and measured, spreading outward with a strange steadiness. People in the square didn't freeze, but their movements changed. One man slowed down when he lifted a crate. Another woman hesitated while stepping off the curb. Several people looked down at their watches at the same time, their expressions tight and unreadable.

No one spoke.

Elénore stepped off the bus with her suitcase and stood still for a moment, watching the town resume its motion. The bells faded away, leaving behind a silence that felt deliberate. She had the uneasy sense that she had arrived somewhere unlike anywhere else.

Her grandfather's house stood near the outer edge of town, far enough that the tower was mostly obscured by other buildings. Henri Edouard greeted her with a nod and a brief embrace. He looked thinner than she remembered, his face lined sharply, his eyes restless.

"You saw it," he said, not bothering to specify what he meant.

"The tower," Elénore replied.

Henri nodded. "Everyone sees it. Not everyone looks."

That night, Elénore slept poorly. The bells rang at intervals she couldn't predict, sometimes close together, sometimes spaced far apart. Each time they sounded, she woke with the sense of having been interrupted mid-thought. As if sleep itself had been cut short rather than ended.

Over the next week, she began to notice patterns. People checked their watches constantly, even when there was no obvious reason to. Conversations were polite but cautious, rarely straying into anything personal or emotional. Arguments never escalated. Voices never rose. Disagreements dissolved before they could take shape.

Elénore wandered around the town during the day, circling closer to the clock tower without realizing she was doing it. The closer she came, the stronger the air felt, thick with warmth and the faint metallic smell of old machinery. The sound of the bells lingered here longer than usual, almost as if the stone itself held onto it. She pressed her palm briefly against the tower's stone and felt a subtle vibration beneath her skin, like a pulse.

At the base of the tower, she found a sealed metal door set into the stone. Its surface was scratched and scarred, layered with marks that looked deliberate rather than random. Words had been carved into it at different times, in different hands, some nearly erased by age.

Keep the hours.
Order is mercy.
Forgive me.

She stepped back, unsettled.

At the town library, Elénore found records that filled in the gaps no one would speak about. Long ago, Ville Du Clocher had been divided by violent disputes. Families fought families. The town fractured into factions that refused to share land, labor, or time itself. Church bells once rang not to mark hours but to signal danger.

Then the records changed tone. A new council formed. The tower was commissioned. Timekeeping became law.

The man credited with the tower's design appeared again and again in the margins of documents, sometimes praised, sometimes struck through. His name appeared once in full and then never again.

When Elénore asked her grandfather about him, Henri sat down heavily.

"He believed time could fix us," he said. "If everyone lived inside the same structure, the same rhythm, no one would step out of line."

"And it worked," Elénore said.

Henri's mouth tightened. "For a while."

Henri kept an old pocket watch in his coat, one he never wore. One evening, Elénore examined it more closely and noticed something weird about it. The glass was cracked, but the damage had been done from the inside out.

Later that night, unable to sleep, she heard a slight scraping sound. It was coming from Henri's watch now resting on her desk. When she picked it up, she saw that markings had appeared along the inner casing, pressed deep into the metal with uneven pressure, as if made quickly.

She did not read them all at once. She read them over several nights, deciphering cramped writing and overlapping entries. The watch was not speaking to her. It was remembering.

The entries told the story the records avoided. The tower had not been powered by machinery alone. The designer had bound his own spirit to a construct he called the heart, a mechanism meant to anchor time itself. The heart regulated the bells, the watches, the town's rhythm. It was not supposed to consume anything.

But it did.

The system required fuel. Not hours, but lives measured in fractions. Each watch drew imperceptible amounts of time from its wearer, feeding the heart. The sacrifice was meant to be spread thin, unnoticed.

Over generations, the demand grew.

Henri fell ill soon after Elénore finished reading the last entry. His strength faded quickly, as though something had finally noticed him. On his final night, he pressed the watch into her hand.

"Our family was meant to observe," he whispered. "Not to obey."

When he died, the bells rang long past dawn.

Grief sharpened Elénore's resolve. She returned to the tower the following night, determined to enter. The door did not yield. No amount of force or pleading opened it.

It was the watch that revealed the key.

Hidden beneath the loose floorboard in Henri's room, she found a narrow iron key wrapped in cloth, warm to the touch. Etched into its surface were the same words carved into the tower door:

Keep the hours.
Order is mercy.
Forgive me.

The lock resisted, then turned.

Inside, the tower was alive with sound. Gears groaned and shifted, chains rattled, and the bells above trembled with restrained force. As Elénore climbed, words began to appear on the stone walls, scratched into existence before her eyes.

I wanted peace.
I didn't know how to stop.

At the tower's heart, she finally saw it.

The heart was not organic, but it moved like something alive. Golden light pulsed through interlocking plates of metal, each beat uneven, strained. The air around it shimmered with heat.

The spirit did not fully manifest. Instead, its presence was everywhere, etched into walls, vibrating through gears, echoing through the bells.

"You are failing," Elénore said aloud.

Yes, the walls replied.

The truth was clear now. The heart was collapsing, demanding more time than the town could give. Soon, it would take everything.

Elénore stepped forward and placed her hand against the core. It burned, not with heat but with weight, pressing years and memories into her mind. She saw the town's past, its violence, its desperation. She saw the moment the designer realized what he had done and chose to stay rather than dismantle his creation.

"I will take your place," she said.

No, came the response, immediate and fractured.

"I am not asking."

She locked the key into the heart.

The bells rang once, violently, and then fell silent.

The bright light dimmed, then surged, and finally settled. The walls went blank. The spirit unraveled, finally released from its prison.

When morning came, the watches across Ville Du Clocher stopped. People woke up feeling lighter, disoriented, but alive. Time moved freely again.

High above them, Elénore stood within the tower, bound by nothing but choice, holding the hours steady so no one else would ever have to again.

The Courage to Act

The Missing Pipsqueak

by Hazel Rallen and

Autumn Mooney

Ridgeline Montessori

Okay, settle down. I'm going to tell you a story about two bunnies and their pet human. Let's get started.

Chapter 1

The Mighty Carrot and his assistant, Dust Bunny the Magnificent, were about to do their favorite trick.

"And now we will do our favorite trick!" shouted the Mighty Carrot and Dust Bunny the Magnificent.

The Mighty Carrot pulled off his hat.

"I would like to introduce to you my pet human, Pipsqueak."

And then he reached into his hat and pulled out a human. Pipsqueak was bigger than most of the creatures in the audience, but somehow, he fit in the hat. That's the magic bit.

The audience was clapping, and Pipsqueak was walking around looking at all their little props and stuff. The Mighty Carrot and Dust Bunny the Magnificent were so distracted bowing, they didn't notice that Pipsqueak disappeared behind the curtains.

After the crowd left, Dust Bunny said, "Okay, Pipsqueak, they're gone. You can come out now." (Pipsqueak was sometimes afraid of the crowd.) When Pipsqueak did not emerge, Dust Bunny told the Mighty Carrot, "Mighty Carrot, I can't find Pipsqueak!"

"Did you try calling?" said the Mighty Carrot.

"Yes, I called a whole bunch!" squeaked Dust Bunny.

"Did you look under all the tables?" asked the Mighty Carrot.

"Not yet. I'll go do that."

A bit later, Dust Bunny came back.

"I can't find Pipsqueak anywhere," declared Dust Bunny.

By now, the Mighty Carrot was beginning to get a little worried. Pipsqueak had never disappeared before, except that time he got shut in the magical mailbox and got sent to China, and they had to go find him.

"Let's take a trip to China to see if he went there," said the Mighty Carrot. "He might have missed one of his friends he met there."

"Yeah, let's try it," said Dust Bunny the Magnificent.

"We'd better start packing right away," said the Mighty Carrot.

Just as the Mighty Carrot was walking into his bedroom, he heard a little peep, and there was Pipsqueak under the bed.

"Dust Bunny!" shouted the Mighty Carrot.

"Don't distract me. I've only put in one pair of magic clothes," shouted Dust Bunny the Magnificent.

"Well, you can put those things back because I found Pipsqueak under my bed!" shouted the Mighty Carrot.

"What?!" screamed Dust Bunny.

Pipsqueak made another "peep" and ran back under the bed.

The next day at the magic show, they'd just finished and everyone was getting up to go, when a mouse wearing a suit came up to them.

"The King has sent a message that you are invited to the Royal Ball at the palace next week, on Friday at two o'clock sharp." And then he left.

Chapter 2

Next week at 2:00 sharp on Friday, Dust Bunny the Magnificent and the Mighty Carrot arrived at the palace with Pipsqueak. When they got inside, they saw lots of creatures with top hats, and Dust Bunny had to keep himself from taking people's top hats off to see if something was inside.

They talked a bit and got some food while Pipsqueak wandered off. They planned to meet back at the entrance at 5:00 when they were ready to go. At 5:00 the Mighty Carrot and Dust Bunny the Magnificent met at the doors. They waited quite a bit until the clock turned to 6:00. Pipsqueak still had not arrived.

"Gee, I thought Pipsqueak got the message," said the Mighty Carrot.

"Maybe he got lost. This is an awfully big place with a lot of creatures," said Dust Bunny the Magnificent.

"You should go look for him," suggested the Mighty Carrot.

"Sure, I will," said Dust Bunny the Magnificent.

Dust Bunny walked off into the crowd. At 8:00 Dust Bunny came back.

"Did you find him?" asked the Mighty Carrot.

"No, he simply isn't here. He's disappeared like a rabbit down a hole," said Dust Bunny.

"You know who this job is for?" said the Mighty Carrot.

"Who?" asked Dust Bunny the Magnificent.

"The police, of course!" shouted the Mighty Carrot.

Chapter 3

When the police arrived, there was only one officer. He was a guinea pig named Agent Squeakerton. Squeakerton started by asking some questions.

"Where was he last seen? What was he wearing? What did he look like? Did he have anything valuable on him?"

The Mighty Carrot answered: "He was last seen under the table around the snack area. He was wearing a purple shirt, red jeans, and a leash. He has a red mohawk. The only thing anyone would want to steal is the golden necklace he wears with a tracker in it, but we took it out because we thought he didn't need the tracker anymore," said Mighty Carrot.

They went over to the snack table. Agent Squeakerton pulled out a magnifying glass and some powder. He poured the powder under the table. The Mighty Carrot and Dust Bunny knew he was looking for paw prints or footprints of the creature who might have taken Pipsqueak, or Pipsqueak's fingerprints. But there was nothing, no paw prints or Pipsqueak's fingerprints.

"Are you sure he was here?" asked Agent Squeakerton.

"Yes, I'm absolutely paw-sitive," said the Mighty Carrot.

Next, Agent Squeakerton poured the powder on the table (the food had been taken away) but all they could see was a place where guinea pig food had covered up something. The bunnies looked at the guinea pig food and then at Agent Squeakerton, the guinea pig.

"That's odd, there weren't any guinea pigs at the party tonight," whispered the Mighty Carrot.

"You're right, there weren't," whispered Dust Bunny the Magnificent.

They both looked at Agent Squeakerton again.

"You know what I think?" said Agent Squeakerton.

"What?" asked Dust Bunny the Magnificent.

"I think that Pipsqueak ran away and he'll come back a bit later and you shouldn't worry."

"I think he's gone mad," whispered the Mighty Carrot to Dust Bunny the Magnificent.

"Okay, we'll go home and read a book or play cards," said Dust Bunny the Magnificent.

"What are you doing?" whispered the Mighty Carrot. "We're not going to just give up!"

"Just go with it," whispered Dust Bunny. "We can look for Pipsqueak after he leaves. Clearly this police officer is no help to us, and he seems very suspicious himself."

"Yeah, we will go home now, and we won't worry about it at all," agreed the Mighty Carrot.

Agent Squeakerton left.

Afterward, the bunnies went home to sleep and planned to look for Pipsqueak in the morning. The next morning they went out to look for Pipsqueak.

"We'll go to the town square. There are lots of animals there who might have seen Pipsqueak. Pipsqueak is very big," suggested the Mighty Carrot.

"Good idea," agreed Dust Bunny the Magnificent.

At the Town Square, the bunnies walked around looking for suspects and critters who might be able to help them. But no one had seen any big humans.

They called for Pipsqueak. After that didn't work they kept walking around and calling every now and then, and asking if anyone had seen Pipsqueak. After a bit they heard trumpets.

Everyone quickly got to the side because everyone knew what trumpets meant.

"Long Live King Hampton," shouted one creature in the crowd.

"Hey, you say that after WE say 'All bow down to the king'" shouted the guards. "All bow down to the king!"

Everyone bowed.

After they could stand up again, Dust Bunny whispered, "Let's go follow the king. Maybe he has seen Pipsqueak or can put up signs for us or something."

"Yeah!" agreed the Mighty Carrot.

So they chased after the king, staying behind some critters so no one saw them. When they finally got to the palace, King Hampton (who is a hamster) had already gone in. The two bunnies walked up to the guard of the moat.

"We would like to see King Hampton," said the Mighty Carrot.

"Is he expecting you?" the guard asked.

"No, but we're expecting to see him," said Dust Bunny the Magnificent.

"Well, let's see your ID cards," said the guard.

"We're bunnies, we don't have them," said the Mighty Carrot.

"Oh, right. I forgot. I'm a mouse, I don't have one either," said the guard.

"How could you forget?" said one of the guards behind the mouse guard.

"Fine, you can go see the king," said the mouse guard.

Chapter 4

In the castle there were lots of pictures and sparkly stuff.

"I think hamsters like sparkly stuff," said Dust Bunny right after that they walked into the King's throne room, which had lots of sparkly and shiny stuff.

King Hampton said, "Hampsters do like sparkly stuff."

"So, what brings you here?" asked the king, in a more king-like voice.

"We came to ask if you had seen a rather large and odd creature. It basically has no hair except for a pinch on top of its head. It is called a human. Ever heard of one?"

"Have you ever heard of realistic life? Of course I've heard of one—wait—what are they called again? Hubibugs?" guessed King Hampton.

"You got the first letter right, but they're called 'humans,'" corrected Dust Bunny.

"Oh, right, I definitely knew that," said King Hampton.

"Anyway, have you seen one?" asked the Mighty Carrot.

"No, but I can ask my guards that patrol the town every half a minute," the king said, "or check my cameras that record everything except at lunch time, but then my guards are patrolling every half a minute. Oh, wait, did I already say that? I think I already said that."

"Great, let's get going. We only have our whole life," said Dust Bunny the Magnificent.

"First check the guards' memory," said the king.

Three guards were called in. He asked the guards what they saw. The first guard said he saw someone rob the flower shop.

"Not helpful," whispered the Mighty Carrot.

The second guard said he saw a rat fall down the sewer pipe.

"Also, not helpful," whispered the Mighty Carrot again.

The third guard said he saw a guinea pig with a rather big bag that kept moving go into an abandoned building with only spiders living in it.

"Helpful!" whispered the Mighty Carrot.

"Okay, let's check the cameras," said the king. "Since we heard that helpful info from the three guards, let's check the three abandoned building cameras."

"I think that King Hampton should be called the king of the threes," whispered Dust Bunny.

King Hampton took them over to a place with a sign that said "The Three Abandoned Building Cameras" on it. On a tape replaying the day Pipsqueak disappeared, they saw the spiders lead the guinea pig to a secret cave.

"Now let's look at the other two cameras," said King Hampton.

"Sorry, we have to go! Byyye!" yelled the Mighty Carrot .

The abandoned building was very much abandoned.

"This place is very abandoned," said Dust Bunny.

"How are we going to find Pipsqueak here?" groaned the Mighty Carrot.

"He went that way," whispered a spider and pointed to a tunnel.

"Let's go!" said the Mighty Carrot.

"Thanks, spider," yelled Dust Bunny.

"Anytime," said the spider.

The bunnies ran down the tunnel. At the end of the tunnel there was a big cave. In it was Pipsqueak and a guinea pig!

"Agent Squeakerton!" said Dust Bunny.

"Yes, it is me, Agent Squeakerton," said Agent Squeakerton.

"Then why aren't you wearing your police outfit?" asked Dust Bunny the Magnificent.

"I am just a normal guinea pig named Jimston," he answered. "I just need to sell this human. I'll get a whole bunch of money for it!"

"That's why he was so suspicious about the missing person crime!" whispered Dust Bunny the Magnificent.

"Don't get distracted," whispered the Mighty Carrot. "We need to kick his butt. On the count of three: one, two, three, ATTACK!" yelled the Mighty Carrot.

And with that, the bunnies were upon him.

"Ha ha! I kicked his butt!" yelled the Mighty Carrot.

"Fine, I surrender," yelled Jimston.

Then they untied Pipsqueak and went home and lived happily ever after!

Rose and the Fairy

by Edmund Titus

Bridge Charter Academy

Chapter 1

It was a pretty normal day at the Titus house. Edmund was making cereal. (He was extremely bad at cooking, but even he couldn't ruin cold cereal.) The two girls, Rose and Flora, were playing hide-and-seek. Next door, Roy was snoring. He was a bad guy. Edmund's mom and dad were out shopping.

After breakfast, Rose read a fairy tale and wondered about fairies and dragons. She wondered if she might meet one someday. I should note that Rose was somewhat younger than Edmund and Flora. While they were both eleven, Rose was only seven.

Rose asked Edmund and Flora if she could meet a fairy tale creature when she was a grown-up. Edmund burst out laughing, but Flora gave him a look that quite plainly said, "Shut up." Edmund had been given this look many times in the past, and he knew to obey it. He stopped laughing, but it was too late. Rose burst into tears and ran into her room.

Chapter 2

While Rose was in her room, Edmund and Flora had the Talk About Why We Do Not Make Fun of Younger Kids. Rose was sobbing into her pillow. She was angry at Edmund for laughing at her.

Just as she was beginning to calm down, she heard a voice coming from behind the window.

"For the last time, open the window!"

Rose didn't know what to do. It might be one of Roy's tricks. But the voice didn't sound like Roy. In fact, it sounded a lot like her own. She decided to take a chance and open it. If it was Roy, she could call Edmund for help.

As she opened the window, a small light flashed through. It landed on Rose's dresser and began to disperse. When it cleared, there stood a little fairy not more than an inch tall.

"We need your help in Fairyland," she said.

Rose stood there in shock. She had never doubted for a second that fairies were real, but having one right on her dresser was still quite surprising.

"What do you want me to do?" she asked. "And why haven't I heard of you?"

"Fairies only appear to those who believe in them," said the fairy. "Now come with me. I will shrink you down so that you may enter Fairyland, and I will tell you what you must do when we get there."

Now, Rose was not very brave. But the experience filled her with determination. She took a deep breath.

"Okay," she said.

The fairy sprinkled some dust on Rose, who shrunk down to the size of a fairy. Then the fairy took her hand and flew off with her.

Chapter 3

By now, Roy had woken up. He had overslept because his alarm clock was still broken from yesterday. (He had smashed it against the wall when it rang and hadn't gotten around to fixing it.)

Just as he had poured the milk into his cereal, he saw a little golden light fly past his window. Out of curiosity, he chased after it. He was led through bushes, over hills, and even through a shallow river. Once he tripped and fell, tumbling into a ditch. He almost lost the light when that happened. But he kept on chasing it.

As you have probably guessed, the light was the fairy carrying Rose.

"We intentionally picked an isolated place for Fairyland so that so that no one finds us unless we want them to," the fairy explained.

"Who don't you want to find you?" Rose asked.

"Well, most humans, for one," replied the fairy. "But also goats. Those things would eat the entire place if they wanted."

"Why humans?" asked Rose.

"Because they would destroy our entire civilization," said the fairy.

They came to a deep ravine that fell into a river. Upon closer inspection, Rose realized that the ravine was actually a wide hole that stretched twenty feet around, and at one inch tall, it felt like a thousand. At the center of the hole, a small patch of land stood level with the place Rose and the fairy were standing. On that patch of land was a little bush.

"That bush hides the entrance to Fairyland," said the fairy. "From there, I will tell you what to do."

The fairy carried Rose over the gap to the bush. Inside the bush, Rose discovered a little door.

"Is this the entrance?" asked Rose.

"Yes," said the fairy. "Now listen closely, for I am about to explain what you are to do. There is a dragon threatening our race. It has been trying to destroy us for years. There is a secret tunnel under Fairyland. It leads to the dragon's nest.

When we get there, I am going to enlarge you back to your normal size. After that, I want you to take care of it."

"You want me to kill it?" asked Rose in dismay.

"Of course not," said the fairy. "Your kind can't kill dragons. I just want you to knock it out and take it someplace where it won't bother us for a while."

And so they entered Fairyland. However, not ten yards from all this, Roy stood up. He had heard everything.

Chapter 4

Roy suddenly understood. It all made sense to him now. He had figured out what you have known since the start: he was in a fairy tale.

"That little brat!" he said. "That wasn't any old dot! It was a fairy that I was chasing this whole time! And if those two think they're gonna carry out their little scheme, they got another thing coming. I'll tell the dragon. That'll put a stop to all this!"

He quickly found out that this was easier said than done. He couldn't jump that far, and if he tried, he'd fall into the river. He tried to use a tree branch to catapult. After his concussion healed, he tried making a bridge out of twigs. The only reason he didn't fall in was because a deer tried to walk on it. He used some stronger branches. This time he made it across, but the bridge broke as soon as he got off.

He didn't care, though. He began stomping on the bush as hard as he could. It was hard work. Finally, the bush was reduced to a pile of leaves and a rock.

"You won't destroy it that way," said a voice behind him. Roy wheeled around to see the dragon behind him. It was entirely black, but only about two feet long. "You just destroyed the entrance. The rest of it is much harder to break.

Believe me, if I could have destroyed it, I would have done it by now. I hate anything cute or pretty or small."

"You're not exactly a giant yourself," muttered Roy. "Though I did hear their plan to beat you up."

Roy told the dragon everything. He told him about following the dot and how Rose was going to get enlarged to her normal size and knock out the dragon.

"This is interesting," said the dragon. "I shall take you with me. I cannot fight a human very well, unless I have one to assist me. Like you."

"Okay," said Roy, glad to ruin anyone's day. "One more thing," he added. "Can you breathe fire?" The dragon opened its mouth, and a tiny purple flame came out. It landed on Roy's hand, and he jumped up in pain.

"Ouch!" he yelled.

"Yes," said the dragon. "Now hold on." And with that, the dragon took Roy's hand, and they were off.

Chapter 5

Rose and the fairy were now walking down a mossy tunnel. The ground was very wet and slippery. The tunnel was very narrow. Rose had to be very careful not to slip so she wouldn't hit the fairy, who was in front, but also because she wasn't entirely sure what was at the bottom and did not want to be there without the fairy.

As they went on, Rose saw a light ahead of them. It got brighter as they drew closer. Suddenly, the light disappeared, and Rose realized this was the end of the tunnel. Fairyland was not what Rose had expected. There was sort of a road dividing two rows of houses. Each one had a round top but was otherwise pretty similar to the houses that Rose was used to seeing. As the fairy led Rose across the road, she noticed every house had a garden, and in each one was an assortment of mushrooms and flowers. She even saw a few roses.

At the end of the road there was another tunnel that was wider than the first so that Rose could walk side by side with the fairy. Rose realized she had many questions that she did not know the answer to. She thought that now would be the best time to ask them, in private and without distractions.

"Why did you appear to me and not someone else my same size?" was Rose's first question. "Why do you keep saying, 'the right size?'" asked Rose.

"It's all math," said the fairy.

"Oh, my friend loves math," said Rose.

"That's nice," said the fairy. "But the point is, you are exactly the size of the dragon's lair, so the dragon will be squashed."

"What's your name?" asked Rose.

"One day, you will know," said the fairy.

"Oh," said Rose.

Roy was having a very unpleasant ride. The dragon was having a hard time carrying Roy, because the dragon was much smaller. Because of this, Roy was very scratched and bruised from blackberry bushes and rocks. "My lair is not much—pant—farther," said the dragon. "And I am glad of it."

Soon they came to a small hole, just big enough for Roy to wiggle through. Rats scampered around the walls of the cave. "Those rats are my servants," explained the dragon. "If you had not been with me, they would have attacked you."

"What could a bunch of rats do to me?" asked Roy.

"Bite you," answered the dragon. "I make sure at least one has rabies every day." Roy asked no more questions after that.

Finally, they came to an opening that was exactly the size of Roy. "This is my lair," said the dragon. "I want you to destroy it."

"Why?" asked Roy.

"They won't be able to squish me," said the dragon. "And you'll be able to move around." So Roy hammered away at the cave with a sharp rock. The rats made an aggressive motion, but the dragon made them stay back.

The fairy led Rose up the tunnel. Rose didn't want to hurt anything, but she knew the dragon wouldn't mind harming her. She got over her fear. She had gotten a lot braver since they started. As they came up, the first thing Rose saw was a cave about six feet high and five feet thick. The second thing she saw was Roy looming over her.

"Hey, kid," he said. "Looks like you're the ones who are gonna get squished. Gimme that fairy!"

Chapter 6

Rose did not know what to do. At her normal size, she and Roy were about the same height. But now, Roy was more than fifty times her height. And to make matters worse, the dragon had burned the exit, so Rose couldn't escape. Roy picked up the fairy and threw her to the rats.

"All hope is lost," said the dragon. "And soon you and your friend will perish. There is nothing you can do."

Roy lifted up his foot to squish Rose. Slowly, he began to lower it.

"Hurry up," said the dragon.

"Don't get huffy," said Roy, "I want to savor this." Rose had to admit that the dragon was right. There was nothing she could do.

Just then, three giant rats came down from the tunnel. They tackled Roy, and one bit his arm. The fairy flew out of the tunnel as well.

"I talked to the rats," said the fairy. "Apparently, they hated working for the dragon, and the only reason they did was because the dragon threatened to cook them. So I promised to give them size to overthrow the dragon as long as they also defeated that boy. And as you can plainly see, they are doing a good job of that."

She was right. Roy had just fallen out the side of the cave. He fell into the stream and down a waterfall.

"I shall return!" he said as he fell.

The dragon breathed fire on one of the rats, and it bounded away. But the other two overtook the dragon and knocked it out. The dragon fell down the same way Roy had. "Wow!" said Rose. "Thank you so—Huh?" The rats had already left.

"They must be going to help their friend," said the fairy. "But now, we must take you to your home."

Chapter 7

The fairy flew off with Rose to her home. On the way, Rose spotted Roy sprawled out on the ground. Next to him lay the dragon. They were both unconscious. Around them were the rats. They looked very pleased with themselves.

As they approached the house, Rose said, "So I guess this is goodbye."

"Don't worry," said the fairy. "The next time those two start making trouble, I'll come right back to you."

"Well, in the end, it was really the rats that saved us," said Rose.

"So they did," laughed the fairy.

No one ever saw the rats again.

Roy had to be admitted to the hospital for severe rabies. No one knew how he had gotten it, including himself. In fact, he couldn't remember anything. He had hit his head in the fall, causing amnesia. Because of this, no one knew about any of the events of that day.

Well, except me, of course. How else would I have written this book?

As Rose was put on her dresser, the fairy told her never to tell anybody about this.

"Why?" asked Rose.

"So that that boy doesn't regain his memory," said the fairy. "But also, it's fun to keep secrets."

So Rose was enlarged back to her normal size. As the fairy left, Rose remembered the fairy had never said her name.

"What's your name?" asked Rose.

The fairy smiled and said, "My name is Rose."

But before either of them could say any more, Rose the fairy was gone.

THE HOUSE THAT WATCHED

BY JULIA THOMPSON-MUELLER

Ridgeline Montessori

Chapter 1: Exploring

The rusted, broken-down house towered over Andrea and Claire. Its shadow cast a foreboding shade over everything surrounding it. Thunderclouds seemed to rain directly over it, creating dew drops on the broken cobwebs stuck onto the cracks. Andrea shuddered, cowering from the wet rain pouring down on her shoulders. Ready to face the "evil witch," she bravely tried to stand tall. But she wondered. Was the witch really that evil, or was it just a myth? There was only one way to find out.

Walking up to the creaky door, Andrea's fist trembled as she reached out to knock. She nervously rubbed her opal pendant necklace between her thumb and index finger. The second her skin connected with the wood, the door's hinges seemed to collapse, and the door clanged to the ground. A huge poof of dust exploded, making Claire and Andrea jump.

As soon as the dust settled, a glow appeared in the dark. Looking closer, Andrea saw it was a pair of eyes.

"Aaah!" she and Claire screamed, backing away from the house. They found, however, that a sort of invisible wall was blocking them from stepping off the front porch. They were trapped.

"A-are we stuck?" Claire clutched Andrea's arm, beads of sweat appearing on her forehead.

"I think so." Andrea's shaking hands held Claire's.

"We have to get out!" Claire started running her hands along the wall, trying to find an opening.

"Wait!" Andrea shouted after her. "Imagine what everyone else will think of us! If we come back too scared to do anything but run!"

"Small problem about that," Claire's voice trembled. "I don't think there is a way out."

"What?" Andrea's eyes darted around, panic-stricken. "We're really stuck." She was as far away as possible from the door, but her eyes couldn't keep from straying to the pitch black, dusty old entryway. She felt that something important was behind it. The only way out. But neither she nor Claire could forget the way those eyes glimmered, sparking a light.

"We have to go in," Andrea burst out, pointing toward the entryway.

"Huh?" Claire wasn't sure if Andrea was joking or serious. "Why—what? Go in?"

"Yeah," Andrea nodded, still not completely sure what she was doing. "Think about it. We know that we can't get out past the walls, or whatever they are, and there isn't another way except for going into the house! Maybe we'll get trapped in there, but it's better than never knowing."

"I guess you're right." Claire sighed. "I don't want to go into the house, though!"

"I'll stay with you," Andrea reassured her. "Don't worry."

Together, they slowly tiptoed to the door and quietly stepped inside the house. Andrea wondered what the darkness of the house concealed. Andrea and Claire carefully shuffled their feet in case they tripped over something.

"Wait, where is the door?" Claire asked, glancing back uncertainly. "It—it was just there!" It was true. The one exit they had entered through had now disappeared, merging with the eerie darkness.

"Oh my gosh, where did it go?" Andrea turned around in shock. But she wasn't watching where she was going and tripped over a small piece of rubble. "Ouch!"

As she sat on the ground, they could both hear her voice echoing through the house. "Ouch, ouch, ouch, ouch."

"Oops!" Andrea clapped her hand over her mouth, startled by the effect of her words. As soon as the echoes died down, the light of a lantern sparked about ten yards away, scaring them both. Andrea and Claire immediately scurried away, hiding in the dark.

They heard a low mumbling as the lantern moved around. A few seconds later, three other lanterns lit up, making the scene a lot easier to see. The lanterns were sitting on the ground, while the shape of a human moved around them. In the center sat a cauldron, bubbling with mysterious liquid. What was it? And, who was the human?

A sigh surprised them, and the human started walking towards them. Their body was hunched over, and as they got closer, Andrea and Claire froze. Not wanting to be seen, Andrea figured that staying still was the best option.

The figure moved right over them. Claire let out a squeak of terror. When the person spoke, their voice was old and raggedy.

Chapter 2: The Witch

"What are you doing here?"

A light unfolded over the head, showing a woman's wrinkled face, looking sad and lonely. Her long black hair dragged on the ground, dusty and matted. She looked lonely, like she was stuck here but couldn't leave.

"O-oh, um—" Andrea's shaky voice sounded louder than she expected inside the large enclosed space. "I'm sorry. We couldn't figure out how to leave."

The woman stared at them for a moment. Finally, she said, "I know you can't leave. I'm trapped here also."

"Oh." Andrea almost felt sorry for the woman. But, could she really believe her?

"We just want to find a way out." Claire bravely spoke up. "We don't know how—" Her voice faltered under the woman's gaze.

"Do you girls really think that I know how to get out after three hundred years of trying?" The woman's eyes glinted with a menacing red tinge as she spoke.

"That's a long time." Andrea's eyes were wide with shock from the news. This woman didn't really scare her. She just seemed lonely.

"I know it's a long time!" she exclaimed in exasperation, tugging on her hair with impatience.

"Where are you from?" Andrea asked. "Maybe we could help you get back?" Claire motioned for Andrea to stop, but Andrea paid no mind to her.

"I am from 3012." She gazed sadly into the murky darkness. "When I went back in time, I got stuck in this darn house. No amount of my alchemy can get me out. My potion is missing a few key ingredients."

"3012?!" Andrea yelled. "How is that possible?" She gawked in disbelief at the woman. "And your potion? What is that?" Andrea was starting to believe the woman was a witch, although she really didn't want to. "Wait. Did you say you went back in time?"

The woman nodded, and led them over to the cauldron. Inside was a bubbling, fizzing liquid, occasionally sparking or popping over the edge.

"It is missing something, but I don't know what it is. Oh!" She excitedly went behind the cauldron. "It says the object is in the house! This is the closest I've ever gotten!"

"Do you know how big the house is?" Andrea asked, looking into the darkness. They had never found a wall.

The witch shook her head. "I've never wanted to stray from this spot, in case I lost it."

"Oh!" Claire exclaimed. "What if we brought the object with us when we came into the house?"

"Hmm." The witch considered this. "It could be…"

Andrea was almost bursting from excitement.

"But it makes sense! It only showed that the object was in the house after we came inside."

The witch nodded thoughtfully. "Are either of you two wearing anything metallic or something with gems?"

"I'm not sure." Claire started searching her pockets, while Andrea reached up to her neck to rub her necklace. But, it wasn't there. She gasped, and frantically searched everywhere around her.

"What is it?" Claire asked nervously. "Are you okay?"

"My necklace!" Andrea felt tears coming to her eyes. "My great-grandmother gave it to me! I lost it!"

Suddenly a spark of inspiration came to her. "My necklace! That's it!" The witch and Claire didn't seem to understand, so Andrea explained more. "The necklace is the secret ingredient! It's got opal in it."

"That may work!" the witch exclaimed excitedly. "Do you know where you dropped it?"

"No." Andrea said in embarrassment. "I know it was

definitely in the house, though."

Claire considered this. "Should we go look for it?" Andrea nodded, and eventually the witch gave in, too.

"Isn't there some sort of magic you can do to mark our path so we don't get lost?" Andrea asked the witch.

She sighed. "You really don't know anything about alchemy, do you?"

"No, not really," Andrea had to admit. "Can we retrace our footprints?"

"That might work." Claire took one of the lanterns and moved her foot from where it was standing. There was a slight mark, very faint, but it was better than nothing.

"Okay." The witch seemed even more determined than ever. "Everyone take a lantern, and let's go." They each grabbed a lantern and set off, tracing their footsteps.

Chapter 3: The Rescue

Andrea, Claire, and the witch had all been following their footsteps a long time. "I'm certain we didn't walk this far." Andrea panted, after walking in what seemed like a circle for an hour.

"Yeah, something must be wrong. We need to try a new strategy," Claire agreed.

"This house holds so many secrets." The witch carefully sat down on a big rock to rest. Andrea and Claire joined her. Just then, something caught Andrea's eye. A ledge that dropped off just inches away from her feet. She screamed, and leapt back.

"What is it?" Claire asked, hurriedly jumping up.

"Don't move!" Andrea shouted, and Claire held still. "There's a ledge right behind you!"

Claire and the witch glanced back, and gasped when they

saw the drop-off. They ran over to Andrea, just as they heard the ground cracking right where they had stood. Slowly, the crack became bigger and bigger, until it split, and the whole edge snapped off and hurtled down. They counted a full ten seconds until they heard the bloodcurdling boom of it colliding with the ground.

"Oh my gosh!" Claire clutched Andrea. She didn't say it, but Andrea knew she was thinking. *What if that happens to us?*

"Wait!" The witch cried. "I see something shiny! Down there!" Her long finger pointed to a big rock sticking out of the cliff face. On it was a sparkling pendant.

"My necklace!" Andrea cried. "How do we get to it?"

In that moment, something lit up in Claire's eyes. "Let me try something."

"Okay?" Andrea hesitantly asked, but before she could finish her sentence, Claire thrust her hand at Andrea. Her fingertips glowed, and Andrea was slowly lifted into the air.

"Aaah!" Andrea screamed, twisting and writhing around. "What are you doing?"

"Sorry!" Claire lowered Andrea to the ground, where she sank to her knees.

The witch clapped her hand to her mouth in astonishment. "You… you have alchemy!" she told Claire.

"I, I dunno where it came from." Claire looked at her hands, which were still glowing.

"You could have asked before trying it on me!" Andrea rubbed her leg, annoyed.

"Sorry," Claire apologized again.

Suddenly, the witch jumped up. "I have a plan! Claire, you lower Andrea to the rock, where she gets the pendant! Then the power generated from that will let me find our way back to the cauldron!"

Claire and Andrea exchanged nervous glances. "Do you think you can do it?" Andrea asked Claire.

"I think so. If you're okay with it."

Andrea smiled at Claire. "Let's do this!"

"Remember, don't look down," Claire advised Andrea as she floated her up.

Andrea was slowly levitated down past the cliff edge they were standing on. She wanted to squeeze her eyes shut, but she knew that if she did that she wouldn't be able to find the necklace. Andrea accidentally glanced down at the darkness below her, and her stomach churned at seeing the rocky cliffs below.

"You're almost there!" The witch called to her. "Just a bit farther…"

Andrea could see the pendant just a few yards away. She reached her hands out, ready to grab it.

Claire lowered Andrea right above the necklace. She reached out, and her fingers just scraped the shiny chain.

"I need to be closer!" she shouted up at Claire. "I can't quite reach it."

"Okay." Claire's forehead was sweating from the pressure. Andrea was pushed a bit closer to the pendant. She grasped it in her fingers and held it triumphantly in the air. Claire drew her back up to the ledge where Andrea shakily rested her hands on her knees.

They headed back to the cauldron, where the witch held out her hands for the necklace.

"I don't know…" Andrea looked back and forth from the necklace to the cauldron. "Are you sure it will get us out?"

"Yes," the witch told her. So, Andrea handed her the necklace and stepped back. The witch slowly lowered it into the cauldron. Immediately after it was fully submerged, the substance started fizzing, and little sparks shot up. It started out purple, but as they watched, it turned orange. The witch reached down to the rough, rocky ground and scooped up a handful of dirt and dust in her long fingernails. She sprinkled it in the cauldron, making a spiral pattern of brown dust curling to the middle of the substance.

"Okay. It's ready." The witch rubbed her hands together excitedly.

"Wait." Claire spoke up. "Where are you from again?"

The witch looked hesitant to tell them this information. "I…am from the future."

"From the future?" Andrea asked. "But how does that work if you're in the present?"

The witch shook her head. "To us you aren't from the present. You are the past. But since you two consider yourselves the present, then we would be the future for you."

Andrea and Claire took a few seconds to process this.

"That's weird." Claire finally said.

"Anyways, can we leave now?" Andrea was getting impatient as the seconds ticked on. She had no idea how long they had been in that house, and was eager to leave.

"Yes." The witch laughed a little as she scooped some of the potion out with a rock carved into a dip, like a spoon. She dropped the liquid onto the ground, then another scoop next to it.

"Okay." She looked very serious. "If you step into the drop on the left, it will take you back to your town, mine will take me forward in time."

Before they left, Andrea noticed a little opal on the ground. From her necklace! She scooped it up and slipped it into her pocket, safely tucked away.

"Thank you so much for your help," Claire told the witch.

"No, thank you two." The witch took each of their hands in hers, and when she removed them, there was a blue spiral mark imprinted on their skin. Andrea just then realized that the witch had one on her hand, too.

They exchanged their partings, then Andrea and Claire grasped each other's hands. They stepped through the liquid, and landed in the grass outside the house.

THE FLYING CATS

BY FIONA STACEY

Fairfield Elementary School

Fiona and her mom, dad, and brother were taking a walk when they saw cats with wings.

The cats with wings were flying in the sky. The cats with wings were looking for an ultra-rare diamond crystal.

A tiny dog wanted the ultra-rare diamond crystal so much that he wanted it all to himself. He was selfish and wanted to steal the crystal's magic.

The cats saw the tiny dog trying to steal the ultra-rare diamond crystal. A superhero pug helped the cats. He blocked the castle to stop the tiny dog.

The pug did karate moves on the tiny dog. Then a whole squad of tiny dogs showed up behind the pug.

The pug used his multiply abilities, which confused the tiny dogs. All the pugs distracted the tiny dogs so the cats could escape the real tiny dog and save the ultra-rare diamond crystal.

Inside the castle, on the way to get the crystal, the cats met a bunny named Bun Bun. They let Bun Bun help because Bun Bun said she likes to help.

Bun Bun and the three flying cats joined their magic to find the ultra-rare diamond crystal. Together they got the ultra-rare diamond crystal!

It restored the cats' magic. Once the cats' magic was restored, they got all the villains in the world.

The whole world became better.

Fiona, her mom, dad, and brother were amazed at the flying cats, and every time they saw the flying cats, they liked to say hello.

Through My Eyes

by Emma Juul

Gilham Elementary School

May 10, 2029

Soldiers on the streets.

Lining the alleys like a forest, stiff as trees.

No one goes near winding roads, afraid of what meets them, afraid of change.

For three years the soldiers have stood. Barking at scared kids and yelling at women who run through the streets. For five years, I have lived here, Asian like the soldiers, but American at heart.

They try to take what they do not deserve. Secretly, we fight against them.

I leave myself to these thoughts as I walk through the early Sunday traffic to buy bread. The shopkeeper nods as I slide five coins across the counter. I thank him and walk out the door. When I leave, a soldier stops me.

"You! Why you have so much bread?" He raises his rifle.

I bow. I remember what my mother told me. "Be polite Melody, and they will respect you." Melody. Like a song. My American name, my favorite name. Me.

"I'm carrying some to a sick neighbor, but I have extra. Would you like some?"

"I no want you dirt bread!" The soldier grabs my basket

from my hand.

Once he sees I carry no hidden weapons he hands it back. "Go! Feed sick ones. Keep them gone. They no get soldier sick!"

I nod, and head for home. I look at the warm bread. I'm glad there is no sick neighbor to give it to.

"You has bread!" My little sister Penny yells as I show her my full basket.

"I *have* bread," I correct her.

"Yes, you do," my sister says.

I laugh. She does not understand what I'm trying to teach her.

"Penny, I need your help," my mother calls.

"Hang on one sec!" Penny replies.

"You learned that saying from Father."

She gets a sad, wondering look in her eyes. "Will he be home soon?"

"Of course," I tell her. I tell her this to stop her from crying. "PENNNNNNNNY!" My mom yells.

"Hang ON!" Penny yells back and starts crying into my lap. Our family is a ship. A storm is coming, and we're all wondering who will go overboard first.

I draw the image in my mind. Me swimming to shore and saving my father. He climbs aboard our ship and we sail for home.

"Melody! Get your sister over here!"

As I walk a still-sniffling Penny over, I finish the image. Father has his arms around me and Ma is yelling at Penny for not jumping in to help. In the image I draw, I saved the day; in the image I draw, I am the hero.

"Mel," my mother says, her voice calm and angry like waves. "Stop daydreaming and go clean your room." I nod and walk away, leaving Penny with the mama-storm.

When I enter my room, I grab paper and pen. I push my sister's stuffed turtle Timmy out of the way, and flop onto my small, messy bed with my mom's old blanket that the cat threw up on, then begin to draw. I draw waves, pointed like claws, scraping the sides of a wooden rowboat. I try to trace my mother's anxious face, but I get the eyes wrong. I try again, curving lines that "kiss in the corners," like the title of a book we read in school. No. Not right. I try a third, halfheartedly. The eyes look disappointed at my failure.

"Argh!" I throw my book on the ground.

"Mel, are you cleaning?" my mom asks in a tone that sounds suspicious.

"Yes," I say without thinking. As I pick up my paper and pen, I hear Penny exclaim, "Mama! I have a bubble beard!"

Clearly the mama-storm made Penny do dishes.

May 11, 2029

I walk in step with Kira, my best friend, on the way to school. Looking from behind, we must look like one of those black-and-white comedy movies Father used to watch. My long black hair and light caramel skin and my eyes that kiss in the corners. Her blond hair, her vanilla skin and bright blue eyes. Our matching purple backpacks bump together as we race to beat the bell. We try to exchange news, but soldiers fill our days and the almost-summer heat blends them together like watercolor.

As we walk into Room 11, Ms. Lane nods and ushers us to our seats. "We will have two unexpected visitors today." She makes it sound like the visitors are not just unexpected, but unwelcome.

Suddenly, a sharp knock. Two soldiers enter and stand facing the room.

"Are these the visitors?" I whisper to Kira, who sits next to me. She shrugs, as scared as I am. The soldiers walk down the rows. They place a hand on some of the kids' heads, including Mark, Lisa, Ruby, and Lee.

When the "visitors" get to the back row, my heart beats faster. But when they look at me, they just nod. I breathe a sigh of relief and turn in my seat just in time to see them tap Kira.

"You! Come!" The second soldier calls, addressing the kids they placed a hand on. As they leave, single file, I glance around the room. All the kids who are left have eyes that kiss in the corners.

I don't think. I dash out the door. The kids are being loaded into the back of a large vehicle that looks like it used to be used as a horse trailer.

I hide, silent. The drivers shut the door, sealing my friends in the back. I think of Kira, trapped in there. What would it feel like to be her? I bet she's wondering where I am. *Don't worry, Kira,* I think. *I'm coming.* But then, I freeze. Will I come? I have always wondered how "brave" people act the way they do. She is my best friend, but would I risk this for her? I have never been one to do things. I draw them instead, envisioning the "would-be" me. Now I have a choice. Go back inside or save my best friend. I could be that person! I know what to do.

I run out and throw myself against the back, my feet on the bumper. The truck starts its engine. I look. Of course the door is locked. Of course. I grab the lock, the only thing between me and Kira. A four-number combo. Okay. I try the year, 2 0 2 9. It blinks red. I try random codes, 1 4 9 8, 1 2 3 4, more red. In my frustration I flip the lock over. *2 9 4 1*—the code is written on the back. I type quickly, then pull the door open, almost flying off whilst doing so. My eyes search frantically. "Kira!" I yell.

She slides around the half-open door, being careful not to cut herself on the old metal and joins me. I half expect her to say thank you, but that isn't Kira's way.

"Let's save some kids!" she shouts. The drivers unlock their doors, curious about the commotion. We fall quiet. Waiting. Waiting. They lock their doors again. We motion to the kids to keep moving, and, after a while Mark and Ruby slide around the door, careful to copy Kira's exact movements, and start to thank us.

"Run!" I interrupt them.

The trailer moves. Very slowly, like it knows.

We begin to help Lee, who is a bit more difficult. She sprained her ankle at school last week, so we must be careful. Lee hops out but stumbles. For a second I think she will recover, but no. We go to catch her, but it is too late. She is on asphalt now, fallen.

"No!" Kira shouts. I feel sorry for her. Lee is one of Kira's closest friends. Mine too. As we help Lisa out, my eyes water, knowing Lee might not stand up again.

The truck stops. "Let's go!" Kira shouts as the soldiers open their doors.

We run. When Kira and I reach my house, I usher her in.

"They're going to be looking for you," I say.

"I can't believe you saved me," she says, as a reply.

"I did."

"Yes," Kira says. "You did something that wasn't drawing for once."

And despite everything that is happening, as we head inside, we laugh, like two best friends without care in the world. We laugh, even though she is being hunted by soldiers.

We laugh, and deep down, I know I will be hearing her beautiful laugh, right here, for a while.

May 19, 2029

We receive a letter. It is written on ruby-red paper with an official-looking signature. Ma gets to it first. When she starts reading, she cries. "Rupert Danes off military duty. Arriving at port tomorrow, 14:00."

I try to make sense of the letter. Suddenly, I freeze. Rupert Danes. "FATHER!" I shout. Kira hugs me and Penny tightly. We chose to fight with America, and now we're winning!

"Kira is allowed to leave our house now," my mother announces suddenly.

Kira perks up. "Can I come with you? To pick up your father, I mean."

Mother thinks. "Yes, that would be fine."

May 20, 2029

As we walk home from the airport, I draw the image in my mind, like I am looking down at myself from the eyes of a bird. But this time, I don't just draw. It's real. Father has his arm around Kira, Mother has Penny on her shoulders, and there I am, right in the middle, with my eyes that kiss in the corners.

The Courage to Be

AUTOPILOT

BY ISAAC CHOU

South Eugene High School

It was a day like any other. I remember it clearly, like it happened recently. It did happen recently, but it also happened decades ago. I was driving to work. I worked in customer service at a regional tech company called LineGen. Everyone in the area always had products from LineGen in their homes, so there were always calls coming in. Something had broken, or they couldn't figure out how it functioned. That was my job there. People would call in, and I would tell them what to do, how to fix their problem. Then I would move on to the next call. It was simple. It was dull. An endless cycle without complexity.

I don't know what happened to LineGen. I look around the room and see nothing from them. I no longer work for them. I no longer work. I only sit. I sit and I watch the world around me. It changes but I do not see it change. I blink and the world I knew is gone. It is replaced by something new, something different, something without LineGen. I am also replaced. I am no longer myself.

I was driving to work, as I said. The road was slightly busy. The radio was playing an advertisement for Cameron Dental, the only dentist in town. At least, it was back then. I am told that it no longer exists. I am told that there are two dentists here now, but neither is Cameron Dental. I must have gone to one of them at some point. I do not know them though. I only know Cameron Dental. I turned the radio knob to change the channel.

I am now driving down an empty road. It is a dark night. I am happy and free, not a care in the world. I am young. I don't know how I know it, I just am. There is a world of opportunity ahead of me. I can do whatever I want, be whoever I want. I can travel out of my small town that only has one dentist and see the world. I can't wait to see the person I will be. I know who I will be, though. I will be driving down a slightly busy road to my job at LineGen. I will not leave my small town. There will still be time, though. I will still be young. I still can now because I am young. I haven't started working at LineGen yet. I don't have to. I stop the car and try to leave it. Leave the car so I can stay here.

When I opened the door it was afternoon. It was the end of the workday at LineGen. I did not understand what was happening. I closed the door again and looked at the radio. It was now playing smooth jazz. I turned the radio knob. I turned the knob further this time.

There is now a raucous energy in the car. I just got my driver's license. My friends and I are rocketing down an empty road in the used car my parents gave me. To travel, they said. To go to college and live somewhere new. I look around at my friends. We have known each other our whole lives. We think we will be friends forever. I know that is not true. I know that they will leave and I will stay. I know that I will no longer know them. I do not believe that, though, right now. I believe we can stay like this.

     Winners Anthology

Right now, I believe that I can have everything. One of them changes the station.

I was parked outside of my apartment. The apartment I lived in when I wasn't working at LineGen. I left the car and went to bed, despite not being tired. I tried to show a coworker the radio the next day, but I only found myself young, no coworker in sight. When the song ended, I was back at home, and the next day, the coworker told me that nothing had happened.

I continued using the radio. I did not like my job at LineGen. I did not want to work there, so I went back. I lived where I did not work there. I lived where I could do anything. I lived where I had friends. I lived where I had dreams. It only ever lasted for a short while, though. Eventually I would remember that I knew what would happen. Eventually I would realize that I couldn't just stay there. That if I attempted to live outside of what happened, then I would be returned back to the path that I had already lived. Every time I used the radio, more time would pass. Sometimes days, sometimes weeks, perhaps more, all within what felt like minutes or hours. I lost track of when I was, how much time was passing, so I stopped paying attention. In that time that passed, I know that I did nothing. I continued my routine on autopilot, not diverting from the path I was already on.

One day, I came back and found a woman living in my apartment. I did not know her. I still do not know her. She said that we were dating. I did not deny that. She slept with me. I slept with her. Whenever we would go on dates, I would use the radio. I avoided the dates as they would always feel uncomfortable because I did not know her. Sometime later, I found a ring on my finger. The woman who slept with me was my wife. Another time I found myself at a new house. A house in a suburban neighborhood. I was told by the woman who slept with me that it was ours. One in a sea of identical houses. I would not have known that I slept there unless I had found myself parked there.

I continued using the radio. I was doing customer service at a different company in the same town. It was a company that was new to me. I do not know if LineGen was still around then. Their products were littered around the new house that I slept in, but they were slowly replaced as time passed. Replaced with new products from a brand I did not recognize.

I did not live there, though. I still lived in my youth. Even as the realizations made me feel more and more hopeless near each car ride's end, I still continued to go back. Back to that empty dark night filled with stars. Back to that car filled with laughter and cheering as it sped down the road. Time continued to pass in the time that I did not live. Eventually there were children in the house. I did not know them. They looked similar to me and the woman who slept with me, but I would not have recognized them as my own. That is all I knew about them. Eventually the woman who slept with me stopped sleeping with me. I do not know why. Eventually the children who look similar to me and the woman that I used to sleep with grew older and left. Eventually I was alone once again in the house where I slept, except now it was bigger, more empty.

I continued on as I had before, sleeping in the time where I did not live, and living in the time when I was young. Every time I went back to the time I did not live, I recognized the body that I slept in less and less. He was an older man than I had ever been. He looked like me, to be certain, but he wasn't me, and I wasn't him. I had not lived the years that he had. I was still in the prime of my youth. I still am, as long as I can get back to it.

I can't now, though. I'm stuck. Stuck in a large home full of old people and doctors who I do not recognize. The children who look similar to me and the woman that I used to sleep with were now adults and had put me there, I was told by a nurse. I cannot live here. I cannot bear it. There is so much pain from years that I have not lived. I must go back. I must try again. I find an unlocked car in the parking lot. I turn the radio and find myself again in that dark, starry night. Finally, I can live. Finally, I can do everything I dreamed of. I smile, open the car door, and step out into nothingness.

MYSELF, TRULY

BY KENDALL MOELLER

Elmira High School

An icy breeze flowed through the church corridors, bitter as it circulated through the nave like a lost spirit. Abigail had no idea how the air inside found a way to be more frigid than the spring wind of Anchorage outside. She'd rather have stood under one of the small summertime cascades on the side of the freeway than continue to stew in the unbearable cold and the curdled shame of sitting there alone on that stiff church pew.

"Our Father, who art in heaven, hallowed be thy name," she kept her eyes squeezed shut as her cold lips formed uncomfortably around the syllables of the words, a familiar vice around her lungs tightening like a phantom noose.

The bodice of her best Sunday dress, which she had been wearing since she was twelve, proved to be just snug enough in the chest to bring her rather irksome discomfort. What she wouldn't have given to be able to tear the damned thing open, shred the faded pink linen, and toss it into the horrible spring slush in the gutters outside in some pathetic display of her triumph.

But she wouldn't. She wouldn't utter a single word of discomfort to anyone, wouldn't dare to rip so much as a seemingly blameless tear into the hem of her skirt, lest she be forced to wear the ruined garment to Mass as punishment like she had been made to when she was little more than a toddler. It simply wasn't worth it to cause a fuss over trivial matters such as her own comfort.

"Thy kingdom come, thy will be done on earth as it is in heaven."

A brass depiction of Jesus Christ hung just below the stained glass window of the church, gazing down patronizingly from his crucifix like a divine critic. The mere artistic rendition of his likeness somehow found a way to have a presence just as crushing as if the actual son of God had stood before her. Abigail couldn't actually see it due to her eyes being screwed shut in prayer, but his silhouette lingered like a haunting vision burned into the darkness behind her eyelids.

She and the statue were the only two left in the nave of the church. Her mother was impatiently waiting outside for her, and their pastor had already retired to the back rooms to conduct his post-mass duties.

It was eerie, the way the silence rang louder than her own words, seemed to be laughing in her face, declaring its own architectural hollows and ominous echoes more important than her faith.

Abigail's lips trembled frustratingly around the prayer as she spit it up, acidic tasting, onto the carpet of the church.

The carpet itself reeked of must. Every step of men's loafers, Xtratuf boots, and the nicest heels that the women who attended Abigail's church could afford caused a horrid crunching noise that reverberated in the rafters long after people had vacated.

"Give us this day our daily bread, and forgive us our trespasses, as we forgive those who trespass against us. And lead us not into temptation, but deliver us from evil. For thine is the kingdom, and the power, and the glory, forever and ever." Abigail swallowed around the lump in her throat and just barely managed to squeak out the end to her prayer. "Amen."

With one last fleeting glance to the brass Jesus, Abigail stood from the rigid church pew and rushed out of the oppressive air of the building. The idea of finding her mother placated with the demonstration of her devotion was a fantasy, so she didn't bother to entertain it.

The fresh air when Abigail pushed the double doors outward was nothing short of heavenly, more so than anything she had experienced that day in church. She caught sight of her mother almost immediately, the woman glancing up to regard her daughter with a placid expression before she beckoned her towards their parked car with a restless wave of her hand. Abigail obeyed the silent command, quickening her step while being careful not to slip on the icy pavement.

Once they had both settled inside the car, her mother spoke up.

"You confessed to Father Smith?"

"Yes," Abigail muttered, tugging absentmindedly at a strand of her dark hair.

"Good, good."

Silence prevailed as it so often did in their relationship, not exactly uncomfortable but undoubtedly tense. The *tick-tick-tick* of the blinker filled the space where conversation would have been, a welcome break from the monotonous humdrum of the engine.

"Stop pulling at your hair," her mother chastised in the same tone she had used the last thousand times she had said it. "You'll damage your follicles."

Abigail's hand fell from her head, resting in her lap as she stared at its upturned palm.

     Winners Anthology

"You have such beautiful hair, don't destroy it like that."

Abigail felt her brow scrunch involuntarily before she manually smoothed it over with an inconspicuous brush of her fingers, hoping that it hadn't been noticed.

Her hair, pin straight and a dark chestnut color for which her mother prided herself in having supplied the gene, was more trouble than it was worth. It knotted constantly, and her ends split and split and split, and no matter how long it got, her mother was never satisfied.

Tangled, oily, too boyish. There was truly no end in sight when it came to her appearance and the hoops she would need to jump through to please others. She had lost track of the number of times she'd glanced at her father's old hair clippers and thought about how easy it would be to buzz the annoyance off and deal with the repercussions later, but they stayed firmly in their case no matter how tempting it had been.

The car came to a stop, halted momentarily by a red light. Abigail found herself glancing out her window, hoping to find something to observe to pass the time.

A group of children played in their warm jackets and hats several yards away on the school field. In the wake of spring break, it lacked any actual athletes and found itself susceptible to the whims of imagination only fully realizable by children. They scurried around like colorful caterpillars in their fuzzy layers, throwing slush and snow at each other playfully and arguing about rules to games that had none. Something strange twisted inside Abigail, her chest feeling tight again as she watched quietly.

An older boy leaned against the chain link fence surrounding the field, somewhere around Abigail's age and seeming to act as a sort of supervisor as he broke up arguments and ruffled the hair of children before he fixed the way their hats were situated on their heads. Abigail envied his warm coat that obscured his frame from the waist up and tried not to curse him mentally when he shoved his hands into the deep pockets of his faded blue jeans. He looked out across the field before he paused, turning his head to the street.

Abigail felt her heart lurch as their gazes met, embarrassed that she had been caught staring but unable to get her body to move to save some of her dignity. The boy blinked once before raising a hand in a friendly gesture. His shaggy dark hair that framed his thin features shifted in the wind, his gloved hand tucking it behind his ear as he gave Abigail a small smile.

She swallowed around the lump in her throat, waving back shyly as the light turned green and the car began moving once more.

"Who was that?" her mother probed, sounding inexplicably vexed.

"I don't know," she began, ready to justify her simple action if that was what was demanded.

Abigail turned to look at her mother, finding her holding a trembling hand to her mouth as despair brimmed her dull blue eyes. A breath squeezed in the young girl's lungs, a certain familiar feeling of dread filling the air of the suddenly too cramped car.

"Oh, Abbie," she started, her voice trembling with a strange tone of sorrow. "Don't lie to me. I know you're lying. I always know."

Her mother's hand that was still wrapped around the steering wheel squeezed rhythmically, the pale skin where her wedding ring used to be now bare to the world as she shakily signaled and made a turn.

"I can feel the devil coming for my baby," she despaired as Abigail continued to stare at the side of her head, unblinking. "Abigail, He's everywhere. Temptation and sin," she hissed the word, causing Abigail to flinch. "You're falling into His grasp, I can feel it."

Her mother brought a hand to her eyes, gasping brokenly a few more times before she reached behind the seat for her purse, her eyes dry and her hastily applied mascara still intact.

"Go to your room. I can't look at you right now," was all the woman said.

Abigail blinked. The car was parked and she hadn't even noticed.

Her hand shook as she opened the door, lagging behind a bit so she and her mother wouldn't have to face each other.

Abigail shut her bedroom door behind her so silently that she had to check that the latch had actually slid into place before she started her post-Mass routine. Her hands shook as she undid the buckles of her Mary Janes and set them at the foot of her bed. She unzipped the back of her dress next, taking her first complete lungful of air since she had put it on hours ago. Her skin seemed to buzz as she changed into a loose hoodie and a pair of leggings. Her thoughts were a mess of shapes that didn't connect to each other, sounds that didn't form words, and that feeling of dread that she just couldn't seem to shake.

The act of kneeling at the side of her bed in prayer was a familiar feeling, but not this early in the day. The sun was high in the sky, though her blinds did much to filter out the harshest of beams.

"Lord," she started, her voice sounding off in her own ears. "I don't know what you want from me."

Her head fell down onto her comforter, the material offering little more than a soft landing as she dug the backs of her clasped knuckles into the sensitive area where her skull met the top of her spine.

"Please, if you're listening, help me." Tears slipped from her eyes, wetting the blanket into which her face was pressed. "I don't know what to do."

Tears continued to fall, the girl's soft sobs muffled as her face began to heat up with the flood of sudden distress that filled her lithe form.

She sobbed for what felt like hours until the air began to change somehow. The hairs on the back of her neck stood on end, skin prickling as something deep in her gut shifted. She wasn't alone.

"Fear not," the presence said without a mouth, without a tongue, without lips, and without a true voice, only the outline of words as they filled every open inch of the room. Abigail's ears rang with it, a gasp escaping her as her head snapped up to face the intruder. "I am here to help."

The figure had no true shape, morphing each millisecond into something equally unfamiliar, unnatural, and beautiful in its vagueness. It appeared to float before her, emanating beams of light that put the ones from the sun outside her window to shame.

A warbling vowel escaped the girl, her lungs burning with bated breath. Abigail forced her eyes to focus on the presumed center of the glowing mass. The urge to shield her eyes clawed at her mind, some deep-seated compulsion planted in her mind which she could not remember instilling herself.

"Speak, dear one. I am Adam, and I mean to guide you through this trial you face."

     Winners Anthology

Though the figure had no face, Abigail could've sworn the being looked upon her with sympathy. Every aspect exuded purity, divinity in its most visceral form. It was simultaneously horrifying and utterly gratifying.

"Please, Adam, turn me into what I'm meant to be. I'm— wrong somehow, and I don't know what to do."

I'm spewing utter nonsense, she thought to herself despairingly, but couldn't seem to stop the torrent of words. "I can feel myself coming undone. I've felt it for years."

The shroud of light seemed to nod, the overwhelming sense of comfort that perforated through Abigail's years of built-up anguish in a single moment being the only signal of the assumed affirmation.

"You have suffered much. You need not ache any longer."

The being moved closer to her, the light emanating from it slowly being recast off of the bed's surface as it perched before Abigail. Every shift and sigh of it felt like a look straight into a world beyond her own, one where she was meant to be.

The beams of the presence felt blissfully warm, like the first sunshine after the dark months of late fall and winter or the comforting embrace of a fireplace.

This feels nice. Why does this feel so nice? she asked herself hazily, with every muscle in her body going loose as warmth encompassed her. *Is this what heaven feels like?*

Her hands were shapeless when she looked down at them, blissfully nothing. When she glanced at her mirror, she saw nothing she could decipher as her old familiar form. Instead, her shape was ever-shifting, like the being's, loose and wonderful like it was shaped to her very soul. She recognized her body no longer. It terrified her; it calmed her. She felt human.

A sick feeling began to eat at her stomach, chasing out any shreds of bliss and instead leaving her with a hollow sort of shame, much like the kind she had felt in church. What had she done? What was she without her shape which she had labored to maintain? Without the delicate femininity of her bones and skin, what was she?

"What have I done?" Abigail murmured, trembling as she wrapped her arms around her body, sure that it would shatter apart were she to stop. She had put so much work into forming her shape to the preferences of others. What would they see when they looked at her now? If they regarded her with disgust, what would she do? All her life was spent making herself into a pretty, inoffensive thing others could disregard, only to be reduced to a monster, all for a few moments of her own joy.

The being seemed to sigh, a long metallic sound that made the ground feel as if it were swallowing the two of them whole.

"I have revealed the you buried within the shell of Abigail," the being replied, patient in its cadence and all-encompassing in its passion. Abigail shook her head back and forth violently, so lost in her fear, that she risked rendering herself concussed.

"My mother—"

"Your mother could never hope to change how you truly are," it declared, the words undeniably final. "Do not seek validation in a place you will never find it."

In that moment, a hand began to extend from the shapeless shroud of light. The motion seemed to drag on forever, the palm of a painfully human hand facing upwards as the fingers uncurled into an inviting gesture that urged Abigail to accept it. It was the first time that the being had taken a definitive shape, and it was nothing short of remarkable.

The digits of the hand were somehow familiar, each luminous vein and freckle intimate in a way just as perplexing as it was comforting to the cowering girl.

"I don't understand." Abigail trembled, shrinking away from the divine hand offered to her and instead covering her flushed face.

There was silence for a moment before the hand slowly caressed her flushed cheek, the brush of knuckles along her cheekbone like a cooling balm as the being pulled the frightened girl's hands from her face. She gasped around the lump in her throat. Never before had she thought it possible to touch heaven, yet here it was cradling her in its palm.

She couldn't bring herself to look up from the floor, simply letting her hands fall to her sides when the being released them to cup her face.

"Look at me," Adam said, and Abigail obeyed.

The reflective surface of her mirror gleamed back at her. Adam's form, still luminescent but now fully defined through solid edges mirroring her own shape, peered back at her from the confines of reflectively coated glass. It smiled.

Abigail's heart felt as if it were about to burst from her chest. How—what?

"What's happening?" she whispered, bringing a hand up to press the tips of her fingers against the mirror. It was warm as she laid her palm against it. "Am I—you?"

"I am you as you are me," her reflection—Adam—she— said as it also brought up its hand in time with hers. "Do you understand?"

No, she thought to herself, but every second she spent looking at her mirror began to feel more and more right.

"It will get easier, I promise you," they said.

"Will it be worth it, though? Me being as I am?"

"It's always worth something to be true to one's soul," they said with a smile, stroking their thumb against the mirror. "Let yourself be as you were meant to be. Do not feel shame for merely existing."

Abigail's eyes never left the mirror, her head nodding before she could process it. She gripped the mirror's edge, resting her forehead against Adam's.

Tomorrow, she promised herself. Tomorrow I'll be myself, truly.

    Winners Anthology

A Splash of Shadows in a Field of Light

by Lily Maierhoffer

Thurston Middle School

The grass swayed like an ocean current. The dandelions were in full bloom.

The sun's rays warmed my back. Another warm, sunny, perfect day. The field was my paradise. The flowers came in so many colors, beautiful and free. The cool waters of the lake were a gift. The clouds were always pure white and fluffy. It was perfect, everything I wanted. Until one day…

It started small. A tiny patch of darkness in a part of the field. As I kept looking, I saw more shadows, though. They formed a trail, and even though my gut told me not to, I followed. What I found was shocking: a forested land of shadows sharing a border with my field. As I got closer, I could feel the sorrow in the air.

At the edge of the forest, I reached toward the shadows. Just my fingertips. Coldness shocked me, and I lurched back. Trembling, I inspected my hand. Shadows crawled up my palm. I jumped, waving my hand to shake them off. I watched as they made their way back into the large forest of darkness. As I began to inch away, ready to forget all that had happened, I saw them.

A small, shadowy figure watched from behind a tree. They had glowing white eyes and looked to be about my size, but before I could get a closer look, They ducked behind a tree. I walked away, unwilling to breach the cold shadows, thinking about what I had seen.

Later I lay in my field, staring at my hand. My fingertips were still cold, but the effect had mostly worn off. For days, I tried to not think about the shadowy forest, but I wanted to go back. I needed to see who lived in that dark, dreadful woodland, and so I returned.

* * *

THE FOREST SEEMED TO HAVE GROWN BIGGER AND DARKER. I sat at the edge, making sure not to touch the expanding shadows. I realized my perfect field was being taken from me, and I had to find a way to stop it.

So I waited all day for the creature I had seen earlier.

At midnight their head poked out from behind a tree deep within the woods, their glowing eyes illuminating the dark. I ducked behind a shrub and watched as they came closer to the boundary. Until they stepped out of its forest.

Onto.

My.

Field.

I was filled with rage. I lunged at the figure, pushing them to the ground. I attempted to punch them, but they rolled out of the way, and my fist hit bare dirt. As I shook my hand in pain, the creature darted away, back into the safety of the forest. I tried to follow but stopped at the edge so the shadows wouldn't touch me. They noticed that I couldn't cross, stopped, and sighed in relief, which only angered me more. They approached where I stood and reached out to grab my arm, but I pulled back. The figure seemed hurt at that, but I felt no pity. After another moment, they backed off into the depths of their forest. I stood there, hatred boiling my blood. In the distance, the sun started to rise, cleansing the field of the darkness of the night. After attacking the creature, I thought things would end.

I was wrong.

The next day the shadowed forest had expanded more, like the creature was attacking back. Enraged, I made my way to the forest, but when I got there, the creature was already waiting for me, holding something in their palm. I got closer until I stood parallel to them, and we locked eyes. They held out something to me.

A small bouquet of sad flower buds.

A peace offering.

I was shocked by the gesture. I looked at the buds; they had never touched sunlight, from all that time being in the dark forest. I took them and held them up to the sun. After a moment the flowers bloomed. We watched as the flowers revealed their colors: royal purple, with white tints near the ends of the petals. Little glowing particles floated up from the flowers as they opened. The figure seemed to smile with their eyes. They held out their hand and signaled for me to cross over into the woods. Instead of heeding them, I backed away, telling them that I couldn't cross. We could try again tomorrow.

I spent the entire night thinking. Suddenly I had become friends with this creature? Over some simple flowers? I tried to understand why, but couldn't. Maybe it was their smiling eyes, or the way they tried to be friendly with me, even after I'd attacked.

What was this creature doing?

I woke up early the next morning, anxious about returning to the forest. When I got there, the creature was waiting for me again. A real smile formed on their face. They had two fangs extending from the top jaw. Despite the fangs, the smile gave them some humanity, making them feel more real. I looked away, still wary. They held out a hand to me, again beckoning me. I felt annoyed since I thought I had made it obvious I couldn't enter that easily. My glare must have unsettled the creature, as they lowered their hand uncertainly.

They looked at the ground for a moment, thinking, before moving closer. Before I could react, they grabbed and threw me as far as they could into the forest. As I landed, I saw they looked proud. I scowled but turned my face away as a searing pain shot through me. I got to my feet, looking around and clutching my side before my eyes locked onto the creature.

I was tired of this—I wanted my home back. My body felt weakened with helplessness and sorrow, nauseous with hatred. My legs swayed as I blinked hard, trying to stay upright. I looked back at the field and slowly hobbled my way towards it. It was all I could focus on, my vision blurry. Everything hurt.

A surge of relief hit me as I stepped into the light. I toppled to the ground as the adrenaline wore off and the pain returned. I turned my head to look for the creature. They were gone.

I stared up at the stars that night as I floated in the lake. The field was getting darker each day, and I didn't know how to stop it. I groaned at the pain still leaving my body. The last shadow on my side disintegrated into the water. I turned my head back to stare up at the sky again. Then it hit me: together the shadows may be stronger than the light, but when separated, the light could still defeat them.

I knew what to do. My plan was simple: get the creature out of their forest and onto my field, separated from their shadows and weakened.

The next day, the forest was even closer. To my shock, I saw the creature running towards me, moving fast. I tried to back up, stretching out an arm to stop them, but it was too late. They crashed into me, and we rolled across the ground. I grumbled and rubbed my head as I sat back up, then heard a giggle.

I turned to see the creature laughing. They smiled at me. I sighed loudly, but then I started laughing too, my anger forgotten. The creature rose to their feet and lifted me up by my hand. I focused closer on them. The creature had star-shaped pupils and a blue tint to their skin. They looked fine, just tired, despite standing in the light. Maybe the light affected the shadows less. I shrugged the thoughts away as I pulled the creature along with me. I wanted to show them around.

That evening we waved each other goodbye. The creature walked with a slump back to the forest. I'm sure staying in the light all day made them tired. I didn't understand why they kept coming to me. I wanted to save the field and keep it to myself, yet I also felt bad for doing so. The creature had a life, just like me, and wanted to exist as much as I did.

After that day we met up every morning by the edge of our lands, and I'd guide the creature through the field. It was nice, and I started to realize how much of a jerk I had been. I could tell our visits were tiring for the creature. They seemed sick often and, since they were a nocturnal being trying to be active in the daylight, they always looked exhausted. Nonetheless they kept showing up.

One day we were both lying in the grass and looking up into the sky when I asked about the forest. They said a dark thunderstorm rained inky water across the deserted field to the far north. The dark rain infected the ground, which grew into the forest. From that came the creature, born of darkness. Everything had been growing since then, taking over the field and draining the life from it. They explained they had no intention to try to take the field itself but didn't think the darkness was stoppable. I nodded slowly, knowing my doom was coming.

The creature asked how much I remembered from my earlier days. I told them how the sky used to be brighter and paler. The creature nodded and frowned. They felt horrible for stealing the things I loved. They told me they were sorry. I tried to reassure the creature that this wasn't really their fault, but they wouldn't meet my gaze. They remarked how the forest was sapping away everything, even me, and using that energy to power the creature. It was like a competition that we were forced to be in. I shuddered at the thought.

Neither of us knew what to do.

Trying to lighten the mood, the creature started talking about what their home looked like. They gushed about the cooling winds deep in the forest and the caves carved into stone. I chuckled slightly, wishing I could see it. The creature asked me if I wanted to visit. They spoke with uncertainty, probably since the shadows made me ill and the forest was robbing me of my strength. The creature suggested that maybe the light affected them less because they stayed calm when in the field, and that if I did the same I might be able to get into the forest. The creature spoke softly, almost as if it thought they would scare me off. It was an idea, though. I had never stayed calm inside the forest. I was skeptical, but I gave in and decided to give it a shot.

I was visibly shaking as we approached the shadowed forest. The creature gave me a reassuring look before entering, immediately looking more lively back in the darkness. I stared at the edge nervously. The creature held out their palm for me, and I slowly felt fear leave me. I took the hand and stepped in.

Nothing happened.

I took a second step into the forest.

Nothing hurt.

I started to walk slowly, feeling my hand leave the creature's. I felt a chill up my spine, and I felt a little dizzy, but not sick. I was shocked that the creature was right. My eyes started to adjust to the dark, and I could make things out again. They watched me the whole time, making sure I stayed calm.

We walked deeper in the forest. I stared in awe at everything. There were huge, blue, shining crystals everywhere. The trees had fruits hanging from vines that glowed and illuminated the tree canopy. No light got through, yet the gloom was bright. The creature led me to a clearing. I was amazed to find that they had made an entire camp. They'd built platforms into the huge wisteria in the center of this clearing. The creature had found such an amazing spot to live that even I felt a little jealous. This also seemed like one of the only spots in the forest where you could see the sky. I was astounded at how late it had gotten. The creature asked if I wanted to stay until morning. I knew I'd get lost in the forest so I said yes. They showed me the ladder to get up the tree. The creature said I could sleep up there while they worked. They were nocturnal, after all. I thanked them and watched as they disappeared into the forest.

I stared up into the deep purple leaves above me. I closed my eyes and listened to the wind softly sway the branches. Maybe everything wasn't so bad. I don't know why, but I felt deep sorrow in my chest. Not for what I was losing or how I had treated the creature, but something unidentifiable. I listened to every sound for a while. I realized my field was kind of empty and looked at my home in a different way. I didn't wish for more or better. I didn't know what I wanted.

When we returned to the field the next day, something was different. The boundary from the field to the forest was faded together. The creature and I gave each other a worried look as we backed away into our lands. I looked into the vast field. Everything was much darker than normal. The clouds had a grayer tint to them. I frowned and went to the lake.

I floated in the water, like I had thousands of times before. I don't know why, but I felt unhappy. Normally everything in the field made me feel safe. Everything just felt empty. I closed my eyes, and the silence was unnerving. I stayed in the lake the rest of the day, no energy to do anything else. That night I pulled myself to the edge of the water. I fell asleep there.

Everything was the same for days. I'd wake up. I'd visit the creature. We'd talk for a while in the field. Night returned and we'd say goodbye. Repeat. It was like this for a long time. I don't know how long. Then everything changed one morning.

There was an extreme chill as I lifted myself off the ground. The ground was the same dark gray as the forest. I backed away, my heart racing. I attempted to stay calm, but the shadows were already crawling on me. Overnight the dark had infected the lake. I could see the shadows spreading. They had gotten more powerful.

The only thing I could do was run. I ran through the home I once lived happily in. I ran like I used to run through the flowers. I kept running until the shadows disappeared. Until my legs buckled. I looked at the sky. I didn't even know where I was. I felt useless as I got back to my feet. I felt my only option was to keep moving. I started to walk for a little bit but stopped and squinted into the distance.

Shadows.

It was impossible. I had been running for hours, yet they appeared right in front of me. These weren't the ones I was

     Winners Anthology

running from, though. It was a completely different part of the forest. I noticed a curve along the border that I had never seen before. It was all one big circle. Closing in on me.

I accepted that I couldn't do anything. I decided to head back to the central part of the field, where the lake was, where all of this first began, where I had spent my entire life. It was all being taken by something that would end me. Once I lost the field, once it was all gone, I would perish as well. All of the running away I did was pointless.

I made it to the field. I could just barely see the lake. The gray area from earlier had grown. It was like a mix of the two lands. The dark was creeping in from all sides. The circle was rapidly shrinking. White faded to gray and faded to black. I could only stand there and watch. While I stood in the last bit of the field there would ever be, I saw a familiar face.

The creature. They had shown up.

I watched helplessly as they walked closer. Before I could say anything, they pulled me into a hug. I closed my eyes and hugged them back. This felt like a better way to go than being alone. I wished I could take back all of the things I had ever done and retry it all. I wanted to get life right. I heard a small sob and then darkness.

Silence.

Then the soft rustle of grass in the wind.

I opened my eyes to see my home. Our homes, coated fully in a light gray shine. I could see the forest in the distance, but it had shrunk. The original layout of the field was back. The creature noticed too and looked around in awe. We saw a flower bud emerging from the ground, got closer, and saw it unravel. Royal purple, with white tints near the ends of the petals, and just like before, little glowing particles floated up from the flower as it opened.

I chuckled lightly. I felt happier, but maybe not like how I used to. This was muted, more melancholic. The colors of everything were duller yet still there. It was calm. A version of our homes that felt nostalgic and fuzzy. I wasn't gone. I was living. I existed. The creature and I looked at each other. They held out their hand to me. I smiled softly and took their palm in mine.

The Courage to Remember

THE GIRL WHO LEARNED THE NAMES OF LIGHT

BY ARYA METZ-HOGAN

North Eugene High School

Everyone in Ashwill believed the fog was permanent.

It rolled in every morning without apology, swallowing rooftops and voices alike. By noon it thinned, by evening it returned, and no one remembered a time before it. People learned to live with outlines instead of clarity, shapes instead of certainty. They built their lives around what they could see five steps ahead—and never asked about the rest.

Elia was the only one who counted the lamps.

She started when she was small, tracing the streets with careful steps, memorizing which lights flickered and which burned steady. She noticed patterns others ignored: how the third lamp on Briar Road always warmed before it glowed, how the one near the river hummed like it was thinking. While the rest of the town rushed through the fog with their heads down, Elia looked up.

Her mother said it was useless.

"You'll hurt yourself staring at what isn't there," she warned. "Better to keep moving."

So Elia learned to move—but she never stopped looking.

At school, the teachers spoke in straight lines, expecting straight answers. Elia's thoughts curved. They wandered. Sometimes they ran ahead of her mouth and left her silent. Other times, they crowded so tightly she couldn't choose just one. The fog crept into classrooms, settling heavy on her shoulders. People mistook her quiet for disinterest, her questions for defiance.

"You think too much," they said.

But Elia knew thinking was the only way she stayed afloat.

One evening, while walking home, she noticed something wrong with Lamp Seventeen. It didn't hum. It didn't warm. It stood dark and hollow, like a sentence cut off mid-thought. People stepped around it without comment, adjusting their paths like water around stone.

Elia stopped.

She reached out—not to fix it, but to understand it. Her fingers brushed the glass, and for a moment, the fog pulled back just enough for her to see the street as it really was: cracked pavement, crooked houses, a town built on endurance rather than care.

The lamp didn't turn on.

But something else did.

That night, Elia dreamed of light with names. Not numbers—names. Each one different. Some burned fierce and fast. Others glowed quietly, steady as breath. In the dream, light wasn't something you waited for. It was something you learned.

She woke with a strange certainty humming in her chest.

The next morning, she returned to Lamp Seventeen—not with tools, but with a notebook. She sat on the curb and began to write. Not instructions. Not complaints. Observations.

How the fog thickened when people passed too quickly.

How the dark lamp made the street feel smaller.

How no one noticed the absence because absence had become familiar.

People stared as they passed.

"Writing won't fix it," someone scoffed.

Elia didn't answer. She kept writing.

Days passed. Then weeks.

More lamps began to fail.

The town grew nervous. Streets shortened. Voices lowered. Meetings were held where everyone spoke at once and no one listened. Solutions were suggested and discarded. The fog grew bolder.

Elia kept writing.

She wrote about the lamps but also about the people who walked beneath them. About how fear made them shrink. About how silence spread faster than fog. About how light, when shared, multiplied.

One evening, a boy sat beside her.

"What are you doing?" he asked.

"Learning," Elia said.

"Can I learn too?"

She handed him the notebook.

Soon, another joined. Then another. They didn't all write the same things. Some drew. Some listed. Some simply sat, watching the lamps breathe.

Something changed.

It wasn't dramatic. The fog didn't vanish. The lamps didn't all relight at once.

But Lamp Seventeen hummed.

Then it warmed.

Then—slowly—it glowed.

People stopped.

They stared like they'd forgotten what light looked like when it wasn't commanded, but earned.

The town didn't transform overnight. Some lamps stayed dark. Some people still hurried past, afraid of hoping. But the streets grew longer. Conversations lingered. Children started asking questions again.

Elia kept her notebook full.

When someone asked her how she fixed the lamps, she shook her head.

"I didn't," she said. "I just paid attention."

Years later, when the fog was lighter—never gone, but kinder—someone asked Elia why she stayed.

She smiled.

"Because light doesn't mean leaving the dark," she said. "It means knowing where you are—and choosing to see anyway."

And that, the town would later say, was the moment they learned the difference between surviving and living.

In Living Memory

by Keiko Weible

South Eugene High School

There have always been gods. For as long as there have been stars and planets, there have been beings guiding them. And sometimes, the gods place their blessings or their curses on certain objects or people.

My family had both, a blessing and a curse passed from mother to daughter. We were caught in a feud so old the reason behind it was long forgotten. Our curse was to die at twenty, struck down by something in our sleep. Our blessing was immortality. From a young age, we were told that if we swore to remain loyal to our patron, we could live forever. If we swore to never forget our allegiance, our funeral would be followed by resurrection, by a life that wouldn't end until we were ready.

18th Century

My mother raised me just outside a small village in Ireland. We were the last members of my family that I knew of. I assume everyone else had sort of faded away over time. They got tired of watching history repeat and prayed for death. I knew I would die like that too, so tired that all I could do would be to pray for release. I didn't know how long that would take. I didn't bother to think about it when I was young.

I had a friend as a child. Her name was Anna. She had a gorgeous smile and eyes that almost looked turquoise when the light hit them just right. No one approved of our friendship, except my mother (and that was only on some days). The people in the village never approved of me hanging around Anna. I was the child of the strange, unmarried woman after all.

Anna was told to stay away from me, but by the time we fully understood why, she was already so close to me and my mother that she wouldn't leave. She found us fascinating. Me especially. Not just because of the curse. She thought I was funny and kind. She found it intriguing that I knew how to make myself look like a boy, even after puberty hit.

"How is it that you seem so comfortable as a boy?" she asked me once.

"I don't know," I replied. "I know I was born female, but sometimes I prefer looking like a man."

The first nineteen years of my life were good. I don't remember many details since time has a nasty habit of making things blur together the longer you are on Earth. But I remember how everything went wrong.

Ireland was not the place to be during the years of 1740 and 1741. What started out as a cold spell very quickly turned into famine. And what do people do when something out of their control happens to them? They look for someone to blame. My mother and I happened to be the perfect "someones." My mother didn't need to eat because of her immortality, so she wasn't affected by the lack of food. She put all her energy toward keeping me fed. I lost some weight, but other than that, I seemed unaffected as well. So of course, rumors started. *Why are they not suffering with us? Who are they? Evil. Demons. Unholy.*

Anna never believed any of it, but she didn't have as much time to worry about me. She had just gotten married and was having to worry about her family. When the people from the village proper came to take care of what they thought was "unholy" and the "root of their suffering," she didn't know.

I don't remember exactly what happened. I know there was blood. A lot of it was mine. I like to think some of it might have been theirs, but I'll never know. I just know that after the mob left me bleeding on the ground, my mother decided to try to save my life the only way she knew how. She dug a grave for me. Anna must have found out about the mob because she showed up at some point. She talked to me, told me I would be okay. She was the one who lowered me into the grave.

"We'll be here when you wake up," Anna said as my mother began to bury me. I closed my eyes. *It will be all right,* I told myself. *They'll be here when I wake up.*

I don't remember losing consciousness. I don't remember being asleep. But I remember waking up. I remember the terror I felt as I realized all I could see, all I could breathe, was the soil I had been buried in. I remember clawing at the dirt above me, tearing at it until I burst through the grass, coughing mud out of my lungs. I didn't know it then, but I had been lying in that grave for five years. I didn't know that my mother had faded because she believed she had lost me.

Anna was the one who found me, covered in dirt and sobbing by that grave. She fell to her knees beside me and wrapped me in her arms. Lord, she was so warm. I could feel her pulse, the movement of the blood in her veins. She was scared. She said that she didn't think I would come back. But she had never stopped waiting. She took me to her home, introduced me to her husband and children as her childhood friend who had gone missing five years before. She cleaned me up and made a nest out of spare blankets for me to sleep in. Anna slept in the nest with me that night, just like we had when we were younger.

I couldn't sleep. There was a strange stillness in my chest. I could feel Anna's heartbeat, but not my own. That's the price of immortality, I guess. I held back tears and hid my face in Anna's shoulder until the morning.

I left sometime after that. I knew that I had stopped aging even before I had clawed my way out of that grave, and I didn't want to draw attention to Anna or her family. I think some part of me also knew it would be easier to leave rather than stay and watch my best friend slowly wither and die.

19th Century

I don't know when the thought of rebirth entered my mind. I guess I must have just accepted it as fact after I realized that there was a spirit following me.

I remember the first time I saw Anna's spirit in a different body. America's Civil War had just ended. I had moved over to the States shortly before conflict broke out. Not the greatest choice in hindsight, but there is always war somewhere. I would have gotten caught in one sooner or later.

I kept myself looking like a boy during that time, pretending to be in my early teens. It was arguably safer to be a young man fighting in a war than a woman without a husband or father. I bound my chest with spare fabric I sewed together and kept my hair a little bit longer than fashionable while keeping it acceptably masculine.

I found Anna's spirit for the first time in a public square in Boston. I had fought with the Union army during the war, and my unit was coming home. Anna's name was Sarah now, and she had come to reunite with her brother, Ernest. Ernie was a friend of mine and had offered to give me a place to stay until I had my life sorted out. I had declined his offer, but he had convinced me to at least stay for dinner. I had told him that I had no family, and he had taken pity on me ("just saving you from being lonely," as he put it). The reunion was beautiful. Ernie ran up to Sarah as soon as he saw her and crushed her in a bear hug, spinning her around. He introduced us and I was struck by her eyes. They were the same turquoise-blue as Anna's.

"I'm so sorry to be blunt, but are you sure we've never met before?" she asked. "I could have sworn I've seen you somewhere."

I shook my head, keeping a polite smile on my face to mask the torrent of emotions that were swirling around my head. "I'm sure I would remember meeting someone as beautiful as you," I told her. I did remember. It just wasn't Sarah I was remembering.

Ernie laughed. "Don't flirt with my sister," he said. "She's engaged, for goodness sake."

I forced myself to grin and said, "Sorry, Ern. I guess I'm surprised. I mean, it's obvious who got the beauty in the family."

Ernie slung an arm around his sister's shoulders. "Of course she's the beautiful one. I mean, what use would it be for her to be handsome? That's my role."

We all laughed, but I could barely understand why. My mind was still reeling with the possibility that I had found Anna's spirit in a different body. Sure, I could have viewed it as a coincidence, but we had recognized each other. I could see Anna in Sarah. The way she stood, the presence she had. All of it was Anna. I had tried not to think about Anna for a long time because I knew she had died. But here was someone who was like her in every way that mattered. That moment was the first time since I was a child when I had considered the possibility that I might not be alone.

20th Century

I ran into Anna's spirit a couple times throughout this century. I knew it was her spirit because both times the brief flash of recognition on her face mirrored the one I felt. Every time there was that same pull, almost like being yanked into a planet's orbit after drifting around in space. And the eyes. I've never seen anyone other than her with that shade of blue-green eyes.

I ran into her spirit during the Roaring Twenties. His name was David. David was a small-time smuggler working in New York. I caught him grabbing moonshine from a stash he had hidden under someone's porch one night. I recognized his eyes, and I told him that I wouldn't snitch if he gave me a bottle. I didn't drink it (I'm not that stupid), but it was a good excuse to have a conversation.

Over the next few weeks, I learned when he would go to that stash, so I took to waiting for him. Eventually, he even let me help. If a stash was in a spot that was in danger of being found, I would move it.

"Ain't no one gonna expect a smart-looking, respectable young lad like you to do a bootlegger's work," he told me.

David never told me where he was getting the stuff from, and I didn't ask. About a year after I met him, he got caught. I didn't see him again, and I don't know what happened. I wasn't too worried, though. I was sure that I would see Anna's spirit again.

The next time we met, it was 1943. Her name was Rosie. The two of us worked building planes together. She would talk about how women were finally allowed to work and how excited she was to have met me. She wanted us to be long-term friends and to settle down near each other someday.

"Can't you imagine it?" she asked. "We could live on the same block, see each other every day. Our kids could grow up together. Do you have a man you're waiting up for?"

I shook my head and said, "I've only ever had eyes for one person." I didn't bother to tell her that person is the reason she would catch me watching her sometimes.

"Well, he must be a charmer if he caught your eye." She laughed, and it sounded like coming home. I just shook my head and went back to our work.

I did visit once or twice after the war, but I didn't stay long. I knew I had to move on. Better to get it over with quickly.

21st Century

Despite rising complaints that the world was getting smaller, I only saw Anna's spirit once in the 21st century. With the turn of the millennium, I changed who I was a bit. I spent most of the early 2000s in underground music performances, chasing feelings and momentary companionship. I wore dark clothes, played myself off as a loner, and tried not to get meaningfully attached to those around me.

I saw Anna's spirit on a trip to Chicago in the early twenties. It was on the Red Line north of the Loop. That was one of my favorite encounters with her. I remember exactly what happened. It was a beautiful June day, sunny but not too hot. I was standing near the middle of the compartment watching the city go by when we pulled up to a station. People slipped past, on and off the train. I wasn't paying attention. I doubt anyone else was either. But then I saw him.

He was beautiful, of course, stepping through the door. He had wavy blond hair spilling over his shoulders and looked around the same age Anna was when I last saw her. He had paint smudges on his shirt and wired earphones attached to the phone in his back pocket. Of course, his eyes were the same, and so was his smile. He saw me looking at him and smiled. I felt myself blush and smiled back. I could imagine what he saw. Dark hair, gray denim jacket even though it was summer. Probably a bit of a mess. But Anna never cared about how much of a mess I was.

We didn't say anything to each other, but when I stepped off the train two stops later, he waved at me through the window. He had the same wave as Anna. I waved back as the train pulled away.

I love that memory. I think it's so special because, of all the times Anna's spirit found me, that was the one that reminded me the most of her. Over the centuries, we had been friends, acquaintances, and more. But in that moment, it felt like everything had led up to that wave.

Present

It has been a long time since the fall of humanity. Of course, the end didn't have a set date, but human life has been gone for a while. I haven't seen anyone else in years. Nature is taking over everything, swallowing man's supposed progress. Broken buildings are filled with things growing and dying, always moving in that cycle. I'm still here, the only thing that doesn't fit in. The oddity.

I replay my story in my head so I do not forget. The people I met, the lives I lived. And of course Anna, although I couldn't forget her if I tried. I don't know why I kept seeing her throughout the years. Maybe everyone is reincarnated and it was just a coincidence. Or maybe my patron brought her back time after time to give me something to live for. Regardless, I'm grateful to have seen her again and again.

I'm going to pray for release tonight. If I am still alive, then that means the old gods must still be with me, right? I can't die from anything that a normal human can, but as long as the gods are listening, I have a way to leave this world.

I'm sitting in an old building. I think it used to be a house. The roof caved in at some point, and the only things living here now are bugs and small rodents. I lit a fire earlier even though the sun hadn't gone down yet. I want to make my prayer at sunset. Anna always told me I had a flair for the dramatic.

* * *

Sunset comes a lot faster than I'm expecting. Golden hour spills across the hills, making everything glow. I close my eyes and take a deep breath, digging my fingers into the soil beneath me.

"I'm ready to leave," I say quietly. "I've lived as much as I wanted. I'm ready to go."

Something in the air changes. "Victoria," a voice says behind me.

"Anna," I gasp. She's standing behind me, backlit by the setting sun. She looks like an angel.

"Hello." Her voice is soft. I'm on my feet in a moment and hugging her, and suddenly it feels like no time has passed at all. Her arms are around me, and I can feel the phantom beat of her heart. I pull back and look at her. She hasn't changed. She's changed so much. It's like I can see every version of her in every lifetime all at once.

Anna reaches out and gently runs her thumb over my cheekbone. With a start, I realize she's wiping away my tears.

I hadn't even noticed that I was crying.

"I remember everything," I whisper. "I remember every time you found me."

Anna smiles. "I remember too. I remember every time you saw me and knew I was there with you."

I cough on the tears. I'm a wreck. "I missed you," I say.

"I missed you, too." She murmurs. She doesn't seem to mind my crying. "Are you ready to go?" she asks.

I look at my campsite, at the world, one last time. The sun is already slipping behind the hills. I take a deep breath. "Yeah. I'm ready."

Anna takes my hand, pulls us close together like we're twelve years old and giggling over village gossip.

"Let's go," she says. The air in front of us shimmers, and I just barely catch a glimpse of something on the other side.

Together, we step into the beyond.